Angels Instead

Susan Larmon

In memory of Rosemarie Wietschorke

"Do not neglect to show hospitality to strangers, for thereby some have entertained angels unawares."

(Hebrews 13:2)

Angels Instead

One

I can't believe I outsmarted the novel coronavirus for two straight years now, only to be utterly defeated just as it finally seemed to be on the way out the door! Eliza lay in her hospital bed in Pennsylvania, trying to remember how she got there – and when…. Nurses and doctors bustled in and out, as she struggled to catch her breath and dismiss the brain fog that was muddling her ability to think clearly. When she was sedated and hooked up to a ventilator, her eyes closed of their own accord and she slipped into unconsciousness….

Eliza's husband of almost thirty years, Jon, had battled a mild case of Omicron himself recently, but recovered without hospitalization. He was not allowed entry into the ICU (Intensive Care Unit), however, unless a decision on his part was required in order to keep Eliza on life-support equipment. That remained to be seen, at this point.

Ventilators weren't as much in demand anymore in 2022, and that was a hopeful sign. The U.S. and the whole world had experienced too much suffering and death already.

Vaccines and boosters were now readily available, but a break-through infection like Eliza's was still possible. No one was immune, even if they had already survived a bout with the virus or one of its many sub-variants. Increasingly stronger and more contagious than the original COVID-19, these new variants continued to cut a swath across communities that thought the worst was over. Evidently it wasn't, and vigilant adults like Eliza had gone back to wearing their masks on occasion. However, it hadn't protected her this time.

—

They say that the brain never stops working, even in the midst of a coma like Eliza's. Her body sensed that death could be imminent, and her dream world began reflecting her fears. She tried to express the panic she was feeling by mumbling to herself about this dream, in the thick of her delirium:

I dreamed that I was the only passenger in a small, private plane.... The young pilot was a student who had never flown an aircraft on his own before! We taxied down the snow-covered runway, and some teenagers returning home from school were walking toward the oncoming plane. They refused to get out of our way, so we had to maneuver around them.

There was a whole line of planes preparing for takeoff, only twenty feet apart from each other. We had buckled our seat belts, but their flimsy shoulder straps reminded me of a parachute harness. Would we have to eject…?

I asked the pilot whether he knew how to take off and land this plane, and he snapped back, "NO!" He didn't seem very concerned about it, but I was! My only hope was that his radio contact would talk him through it. I closed my eyes when it was our turn to take off, and the next thing I knew my bedside alarm was waking me up. Only I couldn't open my eyes for some reason, and I couldn't move my body, either. Did we crash and burn? Did we land safely? Was I going to die? Where was I…?

Seventy-seven-year-old Eliza was still in her hospital bed, and still in a coma. She had been on a ventilator for ten days, unresponsive and in a sleeplike condition. Her doctor, a critical-care neurologist, talked to Eliza's husband Jon about his wife's condition.

"I recommend removing Eliza's breathing tube, Mr. Layton. Otherwise, she could run the risk of brain damage."

"Whatever you think is best, Doctor…. What are her chances for a full recovery?"

"It's difficult to tell, at this point. She could remain in a coma for weeks, or even longer. Her state of mind might be affected, in that case."

"I can't lose her, Doctor! Please help us…."

"We'll do our best, Mr. Layton."

—

Angela began her first morning shift as a critical-care nurse in the hospital's COVID-ICU, when she arrived to check on her new patient – Eliza Layton. Several years ago, when the virus began its rampage throughout the communities served by Grandview Hospital in southeastern Pennsylvania in 2020, each ICU nurse was assigned to a handful of COVID patients. Now that fewer patients required hospitalization, however, a nurse was more likely to be responsible for the care of a single ICU COVID patient, whose comfort and progress became his or her main function there.

When Eliza was taken off the ventilator, Angela began monitoring her vital signs and keeping her doctor informed. "You're new to the ICU, Angela," he commented, when he made his rounds.

"Yes, Doctor. Any specific instructions?"

"Mrs. Layton had been on a ventilator for ten days, and we're hoping that she will come out of her coma as soon as possible.

"Your job is to monitor her closely, and notify me immediately of any changes." Angela nodded, as the doctor continued on his rounds.

As soon as she was alone with Eliza, Angela began to silently pray at her bedside. "Dear Lord, thank You for sending me to watch over Eliza, and to continue to be her guardian angel. Her dreams show that she is afraid she will die before she wakes up. I ask Your permission to replace these scary dreams with happy ones about her past. Let her revisit her memories of traveling to distant places with her husband. It will help her mind to be at peace until she returns to reality."

I will grant your request, Angela, but her safe return to the land of the living is not yet assured. Do not make her any promises….

"Thy will be done, Lord."

—

Eliza's mind started dwelling on memories of her past life – some from even before she and her second husband Jon were married. The city of Berlin popped into her dream, and with it the excitement of *Einheitstag* (Unification Day) in the fall of 1990. She was almost forty-six at the time, newly divorced, and her two boys were away at college. It was high time for her to strike out on her own and see the world.

She was working for NSA (the National Security Agency) in Maryland, when an opportunity presented itself for her to do a two-month TDY (Temporary Duty) in Berlin.

Just one week after she arrived, East and West Germany reunited, after forty-five years of separation! *Einheitstag*, October 3, 1990, was a blowout celebration in Berlin. Eliza was part of the crowd that swarmed toward the Brandenburg Gate at midnight, to see the West German flag raised above the East German *Reichstag* (Parliament). When she heard someone speaking English in the crowd, she glanced over to see a young woman in her thirties wearing jeans and a hiker's backpack. "Are you an American?" Eliza asked, hearing the woman's native accent.

"Yeah. It sounds like you are, too. This is pretty cool, isn't it? My name's Angela, by the way."

"I'm Marion," Eliza said, using her cover name. "Are you just passing through Berlin?"

"I guess so. I'm staying at a youth hostel with some friends – who seem to have disappeared into the crowd.... Oh, well. Who are *you* here with?"

"I'm working at the U.S. Embassy temporarily – checking out their computer security," she lied. Actually, she was doing Top Secret language work, but that was her cover story.

Even the other Americans working at the embassy weren't cleared for what she and her team were doing. She had been given business cards with the name and contact info for a fake computer company in the States and, of course, a new passport with her cover name – Marion. It was the first time she had ever done any undercover work for the Agency.

If anyone at the embassy wanted one of her business cards and called the phone number, someone at NSA would answer with the name of the company and verify that she was an employee there. The only thing that made her nervous was being asked a computer-related question by someone at the embassy, like in the elevator. Her knowledge of the inner workings of computers was non-existent, but usually she was with one of her teammates and hoped that they could answer the question.

"That's cool," Angela responded. *Now we both have false identities*, she thought. "I hear that you can buy a pin for five marks tonight, that lets you ride free on all public transportation in Berlin for twenty-four hours. Let's see if we can get one. What do you think, Marion?"

"Sounds good to me. Maybe we'll run into our friends as we walk around." Eliza was glad that the U.S. Embassy where she worked, in the former East Berlin, was closed the next day.

So she and her new friend, Angela, stayed up all night – walking and riding through the city streets, enjoying the fireworks, and celebrating with the Germans. They finally had their own country back, in one piece! Angela and Eliza never ran into their friends that night, so they were glad to have each other for company. As dawn broke, they decided to go their separate ways and get some sleep.

Angela went back to her youth hostel, or perhaps she just resumed her spirit form. Eliza was staying at a kind of boarding house on the East side of town, along with her fellow travelers. Everyone was asleep as she tiptoed in, including the elderly German woman whose house it was. Eliza was glad to have her own small bedroom, and she planned to sleep all day.

She didn't think that she'd ever see Angela again, in a city as large as Berlin, but Angela knew better, of course. A guardian angel's work was never done, as long as Eliza/Marion was still alive. Angela would report back to God on Eliza's state of mind, and to her doctor on her progress in the hospital, even though everyone knows that God is all-knowing. He likes to keep His angels and saints busy, though, and out of mischief. His angels knew their place in the hierarchy, aside from Lucifer, but His saints sometimes had to be reined in when they tried to influence things back on earth. They needed to remember that their temporal lives were over….

Two

Eliza had been in Berlin for about a month, when a new TDYer showed up at the embassy and in her dream. It was Angela! Eliza pretended not to know her, spiriting her away for a walk at lunchtime. "Why didn't you tell me you were one of us, Angela?"

"Because I'm not – not really. I'm pretending, just like you are, Eliza. Let's sit down here for a minute…. I think it's time for you to know who I really am."

"A spy? I would hate to have to turn you in, Angela!"

"I guess you could call me one of God's spies – I'm your guardian angel, Eliza. He sent me to look after you on this adventure of yours in Berlin. I must admit that I'm having a great time myself, here on earth."

"But…how can you pull it off – as a Top-Secret-cleared employee of NSA, with German language skills?"

"Nothing is impossible for God. That's all you need to know, Eliza. Now, let's get a *Wurst* from that food vendor, and talk some more as we walk. We only have an hour before we're due back."

Eliza was speechless. But then she just accepted her good fortune to have been given a companion on her journey, and she decided to make the most of it. When they got back to their office after lunch, Angela settled onto the vacant computer next to Eliza's, each equipped with a set of earphones. Eliza was asked to bring her up to speed on the undertaking, but Angela seemed to know more about it than she did. "How long can you stay in Berlin, Angela?" Eliza asked.

"As long as you do – so another month, I guess. I understand that people are constantly coming and going around here, so no one will think anything of it."

"Where will you go when you leave here?"

"Home – until my Boss sends me off again… It'll be fun surprising you, Eliza."

"Well, while you're here I'm going to fill up your dance card, Angela, beginning with a classical concert this weekend. Do you like music?"

"You forget who you're talking to, Eliza. I used to belong to the angelic choir, before I was asked to be your guardian angel."

"Cool. How about going to the *Schauspielhaus* here on the east side of town with me, to hear the Berlin Philharmonic play a benefit concert this weekend? It's for the upkeep of Jewish gravesites in Berlin, and I can get tickets through the embassy."

"I'd love to go. What are they playing?"

"Beethoven's *Missa Solemnis.*"

"Perfect."

—

They took the *U-Bahn* (subway) to the concert hall on Saturday, and it was a standing-room-only crowd that greeted their arrival. At the ticket office, they were told that their seats had been upgraded when two VIPs had cancelled at the last minute. It seemed that German President Richard Weizaecker would be in the audience that evening, and they didn't want any empty seats up front. Their new seats were fifth row center, in the orchestra section! When Eliza looked over wide-eyed at Angela, she just smiled back. It evidently paid to have connections.

When the President addressed the audience from the stage before the concert, he was standing a mere ten feet or so from where they were sitting. Luckily they both spoke German, and they tried to fit in with the audience members around them. Their clothing and lack of fur coats or jackets marked them as Americans, however, and not even well-to-do ones at that. Oh well, Angela was a guardian angel, not a fairy godmother!

They decided to stay for the champagne reception after the concert, and mingle with the elite of Berlin. Like Cinderella, however, they had to make it back to their boarding house by midnight, before the buses and trains stopped running for the night. But there was one more Cinderella experience still to come in Berlin….

—

In November, Eliza was asked to go to the U.S. Marine Corps 215th Birthday Ball by her colleague, Dan. The Marine Corps regularly provided security-guard detachments to U.S. embassies around the world. It was quite an honor, and she bought a new moss-green taffeta dress for the occasion. Angela did her hair in an upsweep, and Eliza and Dan met their carriage, a city bus, on the corner. They arrived in time to go through the receiving line of Marines, where she received a long-stemmed red rose. It felt like her prom all over again….

The magical evening included a champagne-cocktail hour, a color guard and formal presentation of the birthday cake, a dinner buffet at which they chatted with representatives of the British and Egyptian Embassies in Berlin, and dancing until 1:30 AM – the new pumpkin time. She hadn't had a date in – too long ago to remember, and it felt really good. Dan was a gentleman, and a good dancer, too. Maybe being divorced wasn't the end of the world after all, although she wasn't about to get involved with a co-worker.

They flagged a cab on *Clayallee*, and arrived back at the boarding house tired, but dreamy-eyed. A simple kiss goodnight and the Marine Ball was just a memory, but a very special one indeed. Only six more days left for Eliza in Berlin, but one of them was her forty-sixth birthday! The girls she worked with, including Angela, took her to lunch on *Unter den Linden* Avenue. Then they surprised her back at the embassy with a champagne-and-cake birthday party.

That's where Eliza's dream ended, on a high note, and Angela continued to care for her as she remained in a coma in the hospital. Angela searched Eliza's memory bank again, and found another one having to do with Berlin, just two months later. Off they went together, in Eliza's dream. It was January of 1991 and the Agency was having trouble manning its project in Berlin, due to the war in the Gulf.

There were terrorist threats against the U.S. participation, and her colleagues were backing out of their time slots because they were afraid to fly overseas. So Eliza seized the opportunity to go back to Berlin herself for another month, and Angela was by her side again. It seemed natural to have her guardian angel with her in her dreams now. This time their hotel was miles away from the rest of the TDYers – on the west side of town. Every work day they rode a bus to the *U-Bahn*, and then walked the last stretch to the embassy. It was frigid cold that winter, and they were glad they had brought their snow gear. Their office staff and the OIC (Officer in Charge) were all new to them since November, too.

The whole office, except for the OIC, went out to lunch every day at a cafeteria on *Unter den Linden* Avenue, that used to be a meeting hall for the *Freie Deutsche Jugend* (a communist youth group). It still served plain fare at a reasonable price – satisfying sausage-and-potato soup or beef stew, with generous slices of fresh pumpernickel bread and butter. It was a peasant's lunch, but it warmed them up for the walk back to the embassy.

Their weekends were filled with new experiences, like a bus tour to see Dresden – a city in eastern Germany that was largely destroyed by the Allies at the end of WWII, and was being rebuilt. The countryside of what was once East Germany was still very poor and drab, although Dresden itself was quite historic and picturesque.

Even so, the city's buildings and palaces showed the results of pollution and disrepair. It was obvious that it would take the whole eastern half of Germany decades more to reach western standards.

—

On another bus tour, this time to Hamburg to see *The Phantom of the Opera* in German, on the stage of the Neue Flora Theater, Eliza and Angela had a chance to talk on the hours-long bus trip from Berlin. "Why does God think I need you to protect me, Angela? You look younger than me but aside from that, you don't look any stronger. Is there something you're not telling me?"

"Every human being needs the attention and protection of a guardian angel, Eliza. We can foresee problems before they even occur. Like the mechanical breakdown that our bus will experience on the way back to Berlin tonight. We will be stuck in a roadside bar for hours with a bunch of drunken men, while we wait for the bus company to send us another bus from Berlin. I will protect you from any drunken advances."

"How will you do *that*, Angela?"

"Wait and see. It'll be impressive…."

The Neue Flora Theater had been built specifically for the production of *The Phantom of the Opera*, which played there exclusively on a regular basis.

In addition to the haunting musical score, entirely in German, it featured pyrotechnics, an enormous crystal chandelier that came crashing down onto the stage, and even a gondola making its way through the mist as the Phantom kidnapped Christine and whisked her down to his hideaway under the Paris Opera. Eliza loved it enough to buy the soundtrack recording during intermission.

Angela was right about the bus breaking down halfway back to Berlin. It was Sunday evening, so vehicle repair shops were closed and their mechanics were drinking away their troubles at the roadside bar. They must have thought it odd to see a busload of frustrated Americans pile into the bar with their tale of woe. When an inebriated, middle-aged local guy started complimenting Eliza on her German and asking if she would like to accompany him home, Angela told him off in no uncertain terms in colloquial German. He back off without a word.

"What did you tell him, Angela? I've never even heard some of those words in German…."

"I told him exactly what he should do with his obscene invitation. I don't think any of them will bother us again."

"How does God feel about His angels using such language?" Eliza laughed.

"You have to fight fire with fire, Eliza. I'll teach you a few phrases in German that will serve you well in situations like this. In the meantime, let's have something to eat and drink while we're waiting for another bus. It could be a while…."

Three

Eliza never thought that she'd go back to Hamburg again, but eight months later there she was on another temporary tour of duty. This NSA project needed two German linguists in the fall of 1991, and Eliza had suggested that Angela come with her. It was all in Eliza's dream, after all, and so she could invite whomever she wanted! They occupied a small office in the U.S. Consulate there, and the OIC took care of computer support and public relations.

Angela and Eliza were like sisters now, seeing the sights of Hamburg together on the weekends. They watched ships passing on the Elbe River, each ship's national anthem being broadcast from the Welcome Point. They attended the *Fischmarkt* on a Sunday morning, highlighted by a huge breakfast tent with a rock band and dancing. Then came the infamous *Reeperbahn* in St Pauli, a street of sex shops, clubs, and prostitutes beckoning to passersby from their windows.

Angela wasn't shy about coming along, although angels weren't really interested in that sort of thing. On the one-year anniversary of German Unification Day, everyone had the day off again. Angela and Eliza walked down to Alster Lake, where all the German *Länder* (states) had set up booths for eating traditional foods and drinking regional beer. They ate and drank their way around the lake, and then followed the crowd down to the harbor for the parade of tall ships.

Before the officer in charge closed down their abbreviated project in Hamburg, he wanted to go and see Berlin in advance of flying home. One of the guys at the consulate who was cleared for their covert operation offered to drive his three colleagues to Berlin for the day. It was only a two-and-a-half-hour trip on the autobahn, at an average speed of eighty-five mph, of course. It was very nostalgic to visit the city where Eliza had worked for a total of three months, a year ago.

When Eliza caught sight of the Brandenburg Gate, she did a double-take! The Quadriga (the golden statue of a four-horsed chariot, driven by the goddess of peace) was back atop the Gate at last. It had been undergoing repairs when Eliza was in Berlin last year, and she had never seen it in its rightful place. She thought it looked magnificent, the crowning touch on an otherwise rather bare Brandenburg Gate. Back in Hamburg, it soon became painfully clear that there was nothing more they could do to salvage their project. It was time to wrap it up, literally.

"We have to pack up all the equipment, and ship it back home before we can leave," their boss announced. By that he meant that *Eliza and Angela* would be responsible for packing up the equipment, while he shook hands with everyone else at the consulate and made up stories about why they were leaving. Only a few specially-cleared members of the staff knew the real reason.

That left the two inexperienced women to deal with the boxes and packing materials for electronics equipment that they barely knew how to operate, much less how to pack so that it could be safely shipped. Unfortunately, Angela and Eliza would be held accountable for any breakage discovered stateside, since they had to sign the packing-inventory paperwork. They sat in the middle of the office floor – surrounded by boxes, packing peanuts, bubble wrap, masking tape, and paperwork.

"Okay, so let's unplug everything first," Eliza suggested.

"That's a brilliant idea," Angela laughed.

They tried to find the right box for each piece of equipment, according to size. Of course, they weren't the original boxes that the new equipment had come in. That would have revealed their specific use. The hope was that using the consulate as their point of origination would facilitate its transport back to Agency Headquarters, with a minimum of questions asked.

The girls were terrified, though, that their uninformed packing methods would result in unusable equipment at the other end. Each piece would probably take at least a whole year's salary for Eliza to replace. So they wrapped, and taped, and used the peanuts as a buffer on all sides, and included a signed inventory slip on top, inside and out – but still had no idea if it was enough protection for overseas shipping. How could they?

After two days of this nonsense, the boss was happy to see that it was finished, and he called in the grunts to carry it out – taking the credit, of course. Now it was time to pack their own suitcases, and make flight reservations – at least for Eliza. Angela didn't need a plane to get back.

—

Back in the ICU in Pennsylvania in 2022, Angela went over Eliza's medical charts, as she did every day. Although Eliza was still in a coma and unresponsive after several weeks of being off the ventilator, she had now been testing negative for COVID at last. That was a huge milestone, and it meant that her husband Jon could visit her in the hospital. He started coming in every day, to sit by her bedside and hold her hand. Her eyes were still closed and she didn't appear to know that he was even there, but that didn't stop him from coming.

"One of these days, Angela, my wife is going to open her eyes and smile at me. I just know it."

"I hope you're right, Jon, but I have an idea that might speed things up. If you're willing to go along with it…."

"Just name it – I'll try anything at this point."

"Did you and Eliza ever share an adventure together? Maybe a trip to a place she always wanted to visit?"

"We had the ultimate adventure together, about twenty-five years ago! We had only been married for several years, and she applied for a three-year PCS – that's a permanent change of station – in Germany. She came home from work at NSA one day, and said that she had gotten a phone call from Germany on her secure line – in regard to the job opening. They wanted her to join their liaison staff over there! She was so excited that she could barely talk! We were going to live in Wiesbaden for three years!"

"That sounds fantastic! You must have a lot of stories to tell, about your memories of those years. Which brings me to my idea…. Would you be willing to sit here and talk to Eliza about the experiences you shared together in Europe during those three years? It's possible that she might register your words subconsciously, and maybe even dream about your adventures. It would help her mind to pass the time in a positive way, until she regains consciousness."

"Do you think she *will* wake up, Angela? I know you're not her doctor…."

"And *I* know you care about her, Jon, or you wouldn't be here with her every day. No one can say for sure what will happen – except God, and He's keeping it to Himself. But this is one thing we could try, and you know what they say about that, don't you…?"

"God helps those who help themselves?"

"Bingo! Do you want to give it a shot?"

"I'll start right now – until you kick me out, that is! Let me just think about how it all began…."

—

"Eliza…do you remember where we moved to in 1997? That's right – Wiesbaden, Germany! It had been your lifelong goal to live in a European country for a few years, and at last all your efforts had paid off. The fact that it happened to be your ancestral homeland was just icing on the cake. Not that it was easy…. Finding a place to live over there was the first hurdle. Remember where we spent the first nine weeks?"

He reminded her of how they were taken to the American Arms Hotel in Wiesbaden, where they would stay until suitable housing could be found.

It was where U.S. military and civilian families lived, who were deploying into or out of the area. The American Arms was a little slice of America, in the middle of a stately German city in Hessen. Wiesbaden hadn't been destroyed during WWII, so its pre-war architecture still graced the tree-lined avenues. An American passport was required for entry into the hotel, but the price was right – zero – if you presented your orders.

On Sunday mornings, the American-style brunch really *was* something to write home about. Eliza's next dream had already gotten underway when Jon mentioned the brunch. "I loved those brunches so much, Jon," she said in her dream. "They had made-to-order omelets, waffles, pancakes, and crepes – with every imaginable filling and topping."

"Yes, and Mimosas you could mix yourself, with as much champagne as you wanted with the orange juice in each drink! There was juicy roast beef and ham being carved, too."

"And eggs any way you wanted them – even Eggs Benedict! For Germany, it was considered exotic…. The German friends we had made sometimes came as our guests – remember, Jon? They just wanted to try pancakes with maple syrup, but they thought it was so odd!"

—

Jon went home from the hospital alone, as usual, but he felt comforted after reminiscing with his sleeping wife and imagining her responses. Eliza herself became wrapped up in the previous life they had shared in Germany, and her dreams continued long after he left her side. She had worked in a building that was off-limits to other military personnel on the U.S. Army post. No one else knew exactly what was going on at the European Technical Center (ETC), and that's the way they wanted it. Her little office was comprised of only half a dozen liaison officers, each with different responsibilities.

Eliza was in charge of the U.S. joint projects with France and Tunisia, because of her fluency in French; and also those involving Italy and Greece, despite not speaking Italian or Greek. How many people actually spoke Greek, other than the Greeks themselves? It was a huge learning curve for her, especially since she was not technically inclined. But she coordinated everything with the engineers on staff, and spent much of her day communicating over the phone or by computer. It was stressful for an introspective person, but she made many new friends.

Jon, a natural extrovert with lots of time on his hands, was perfectly happy to see Germany from the back of his motorcycle while she was working during the week. Then they used their weekends together to travel to surrounding countries and other parts of Germany.

They were each fulfilling their individual dreams, and Eliza was thankful that he had been willing to put his stateside work-life on hold for three years. So many other spouses or children were simply not able to make the adjustment, and whole families had been obliged to return home early from their three-year tours.

Four

The housing department at ETC tried hard to find Eliza and Jon an acceptable place to live in the area, but the Laytons were holding out for just the right spot. They had shipped all their big, clunky, 1970's era, Mediterranean-style furniture over to Germany with them, and it wouldn't have fit into some of the condos they were shown. One small apartment was in a neighborhood full of young American families, with noisy children playing ball in the street. The movers could never have negotiated Eliza's huge double-mirrored dresser up two flights of the narrow staircase to the available apartment – not to mention their massive dining-room buffet!

Another possibility was a duplex out along the picturesque Rhine River. The location was beautiful but almost an hour away from ETC, especially during weekday commuting hours.

There was only one way to access the riverside properties, and that was on a two-lane road with no legal way to pass any slow traffic. If you were a retiree with nowhere you had to be at a particular time, or a tourist just out to enjoy the sights, it would have been an ideal location. But some of Eliza's co-workers who had chosen to live in this area eventually regretted it.

ETC finally found them a four-level townhouse in a suburb of Wiesbaden, and Eliza and Jon snatched it up. All their furniture fit perfectly, and Eliza only had a fifteen-minute commute. The American family of five who had lived there before them had needed large American-sized appliances, so it was easier for ETC to just leave them installed. Even though Eliza and Jon were each allowed one *Schrank* (free-standing clothes wardrobe), ETC just left the five that were already there – four for Eliza and one for Jon. That seemed fair to her. They all fit into one of the spare bedrooms, which they dubbed the *Schrank* room.

While Eliza and Jon lived in their townhouse rent-free, courtesy of her employer, their neighbors had each bought their adjacent townhouses for quite a bit of money. On one side lived a German couple with two small children. Eliza was glad for the opportunity to speak German with them, although *they* wanted to practice their English. They ended up taking turns. There was a large Turkish family on the other side of their house, but they only spoke Turkish despite being very friendly.

The only thing they had in common with the Turks was outdoor grilling, which was not a common sight in Germany. Still, it created a non-verbal bond.

—

When Eliza had met her liaison team for the first time, now in her dream, *there* was Angela front and center as another fairly new hire from the States. Angela greeted Eliza as a previous co-worker, who had already been in Wiesbaden for a few months. She invited Eliza to walk over to the sandwich shop on the post for lunch, so that they could talk privately. She knew that Eliza was shocked to see her on the liaison team.

"How did you know that I was coming over here, Angela? This can't be a coincidence!"

"We angels have our ways," she laughed. "By the power of God, of course. I figured that you might need a little moral support, so here I am – at your service!"

"Do all guardian angels take human form? That would double the world's population!"

"No. Most of us remain invisible, but God decided you needed to know that I was watching over you."

"Why? Am I in some kind of danger?"

"It's just that you might need some guidance during this adventure you're on in Germany."

"But my new husband is here with me, too."

"I know, and that's great – but let's keep my angel status as our little secret, okay? Let your husband think I'm just one of the liaison team members."

"Okay. You're the boss, Angela."

"I'm not, but thanks for the vote of confidence, Eliza. Let's get something to eat...."

—

Angela and Eliza each had their separate jobs to do in Wiesbaden, but Jon was always there for his wife when she got back from one of her four yearly program reviews in each of the countries for which she was responsible. She would share any non-classified details of her trips to Rome, Paris, Tunis, and Athens; and Jon would regale her with stories of his motorcycle rides through the Alps. He had bought a book entitled "The Fifty Most Beautiful Alpine Passes," and he was determined to experience all of them during their years in Germany.

On other occasions during their three-year tour, Jon and Eliza's family members and friends made the Atlantic crossing to visit *them*. Jon's grown daughter undertook the trip in the fall of 1998, and it turned out to be a fateful visit.

After touring Anne Frank's house on a canal in Amsterdam and the famous Delft pottery factory near The Hague, they traveled to Bruges, Belgium, a medieval town on the North Sea, where a phone call during the night changed their lives. Eliza's brother called on Labor Day with the news that their father had just died, at the age of ninety-four.

They flew home immediately for his funeral in Pennsylvania, and Jon's daughter returned to Florida prematurely. As they were checking out of the Albert I Hotel in Bruges the next morning, the hotel's English Spaniel stood before Eliza and looked as if he wanted to tell her something. The young dog reminded Eliza of their family's previous cocker spaniel, Taffy, whom her father had loved. She had the feeling that her father was trying to tell her something through that dog. Perhaps the message was that all was well with him now, and that they needn't mourn for him.

When Eliza and Jon finally returned to Wiesbaden after the funeral, Angela wished she could wrap her wings around her friend in a comforting embrace, but her human arms could only hug her. This was not the kind of memory that would bring Eliza peace and joy, and help her to awaken from her coma with a new lease on life. But Angela knew that sorrow was inevitable in every human existence, and she could only hope that happier dreams would soon follow.

As 1999 rolled in, Eliza and Jon were still in the Christmas spirit when they joined their German friends, the Webers, for a road trip into the former East Germany to the village of Seiffen, south of Dresden. It boasted a centuries-old tradition of woodcarving, including a variety of colorful nutcrackers and the endless sizes and styles of Christmas pyramids. They bought small *Pyramiden* for each of their kids, and a three-foot high, three-tiered pyramid for themselves – complete with a supply of candles to keep the windmills turning on all the tops. The three levels of their large pyramid were peopled with simple carved figures of the Holy Family, the shepherds with their sheep, and the Three Wise Men bearing gifts.

—

Aah…! A luxurious, relaxing USO weekend in May, 1999, just for women! Eliza and Angela were among the first ones to sign up to spend a day in the German spa town of Bad Orb, and overnight in the Büdingen Castle. They relaxed in the saunas and pools, and could even get massage treatments. "What…? Are you going to get a massage, Angela?" Eliza was skeptical.

"Why not? Having a human body is much more tiring than being a spirit. I ache all over…. Let's go together, Eliza – we'll be like mother and daughter."

"Yeah, but I look more like *your mother*!"

"Not by the end of *this* weekend, you won't!"

The beauty salon offered a complete cosmetic and anti-stress facial regimen, as well as manicures, pedicures, and specialty massages. Hmm! In the evening, they feasted on a gourmet dinner in the castle, which also served breakfast the next morning. After a guided tour of the castle interior on Sunday, they could either take part in a stress-reducing outdoor yoga session or enjoy a walk along the paths surrounding the castle. All thanks to the backing of the nearby U.S. Rhein-Main Air Base.

Jon was on hand when their bus pulled back onto the post Sunday evening, and the tired but happy weekend travelers tumbled out. They felt rejuvenated, as you would after a challenging exercise class – glad you went, but happy to be home. Angela peeled off to drive back to her apartment on the outskirts of Wiesbaden. They'd be expected at work bright and early the next morning. "How was it?" Jon asked, as he drove Eliza back home to Wiesbaden.

"A welcome change in routine, and a chance to spend more time with colleagues."

"You and Angela have gotten quite close, I've noticed," he smiled over at Eliza. "That's one thing I'm missing here in Germany – friends."

"I know. We see each other every day at ETC, but this was a break from all that serious business.

"We just kicked back, and left it all behind for a few days. It was great."

"What's Angela like? She seems kind of otherworldly, somehow."

Eliza smiled. "She has a strong faith in God, that's for sure. I think that we were *meant* to be friends, if that makes any sense."

"It does. I'm glad you have an ally at work…." Eliza left it at that, and changed the subject.

—

Eliza's next trip that month was one that she and Jon could do together, again – her Spangenberg family reunion in the German town of the same name. They had originally met their friends the Webers there, since Volkmar also had a Spangenberg in his ancestry. The four spent the whole weekend together – going through the town archives, taking a walking tour of Spangenberg, feasting on wurst and beer at the reunion's barbeque outside of town, having dinner in the Spangenberg castle *(Schloß Spangenberg)*, and dancing the night away in the Knight's Ballroom *(Rittersaal der Schloß)*.

After numerous champagne toasts to all the Spangenbergs who had come from across Europe and around the world, Eliza and Jon were ready to retire to their bedroom in the *Schloß*.

It was an inviting, canopied king-sized bed, and the room looked out on the courtyard of the castle. "Have you noticed that there are two down-comforters on the bed, Jon?"

"Yes, and see how they pushed two single beds together? Each person has his or her own comforter, so nobody can get away with hogging it. And by nobody, I mean *you*, Eliza!"

"*You're* the one who pulls it over to your side every night! And you hang onto it with a death grip, too. Maybe we should each have our own comforter at home, Jon."

Let's see how it goes tonight, and then decide…."

Five

Paris, je t'aime! In June of 1999, two events were drawing Eliza back to France, and Jon came along with her. The first was a choral concert in Paris sung by the German-American Community Choir (GACC), of which she was a proud member. It was a program of French choral works, including Francis Poulenc's haunting *O Magnum Mysterium,* Lili Boulanger's *Hymne au Soleil,* and Georges Bizet's *Valse avec Choeur.* They performed at the American Cathedral in Paris, which was a thrill in itself.

Then Eliza was invited to the office of the SLO (Senior Language Officer) at the U.S. Embassy in Paris. She had met with Joanne before, when she came with her ETC engineering and communications experts to discuss their countries' joint projects at the annual program review.

This occasion was more personal, however, since it was the last time Eliza and Joanne would meet before Eliza and her husband rotated back to the States. Someone else would be Joanne's ETC liaison contact after that.

The two women had become friends in addition to colleagues over the past three years, and Joanne wanted to take advantage of Eliza's being in Paris that weekend to sing with the GACC. "I have to admit that I'm both happy and sad to see you here this weekend, Eliza. You've been doing a great job at ETC for us, and we'll be sorry to see you go after the holidays. Couldn't you extend your tour for another year?"

"Jon would love to – he needs more time to finish riding his motorcycle over all the best Alpine passes, but I miss my kids too much. How about you? When do you and your husband rotate back home?"

"I've extended once already, and I probably will again. We love it here in Paris and we haven't got any kids, so we'll probably stay until my boss draws the line."

"That will never happen, Joanne. The embassy won't want to see you go."

"You could apply for the job, Eliza. You do speak French, after all."

"But I don't have the grade level for it, Joanne. I'd need several promotions just to qualify. But thanks...."

"Enough shop talk. How about you and Jon coming to the Moulin Rouge with us tonight? I can get a discount on tickets, through the embassy...."

"We're in! We could take the metro and meet you there. Just name a time...."

Joanne and Cody met Eliza and Jon outside *Le Bal du Moulin Rouge,* with its red windmill lighting up the whole block in the Pigalle district. They were all dressed for the occasion, not wanting to look like American tourists. Eliza and Joanne introduced their husbands, and they all went in. Cody ordered champagne as soon as they were seated at a cabaret table, one that was not very far from the stage. "This will be the Centenary Revue, called *Formidable,*" Joanne said. "It will be replaced in November, before the Y2K Millennium."

As they ate their steak and lobster dinners, and drank more champagne, the cabaret show began with a giant aquarium rising up from under the stage with scantily-clad, synchronized swimmers of both sexes cavorting under the water, only now and then coming up for air. But the best was saved for last – the traditional French cancan, danced to the music of Jacques Offenbach.

"No wonder no one under eighteen is allowed to see the show," Eliza commented. "Those dancers stuck their rear ends right in the faces of the people in the front row!"

—

Eliza couldn't believe that her brother Laurie and his wife Mira were coming over to Germany to visit them! Eliza and Jon took them to see their ancestral town of Spangenberg, and Volkmar and Liselotte Weber met them all there. Evidently, the surname of Spangenberg was taken by all those who had once lived there, but then left. Hence Eliza and Laurie's great-grandfather was August Friedrich (von) Spangenberg, who immigrated to Erie, Pennsylvania, in 1871. His letters from his family back in Germany were handed down within his new family, and Eliza eventually translated them.

Now they suddenly found a distant cousin in Nienhagen up north, Gudrun, and perhaps the Webers were somehow related to her, too! Of course, some say that if you could trace your family back far enough, everyone would be related to everyone else. But the exciting part is finding new relatives who are living during your own short lifespan!

—

Wir gehen nach Italien! It wasn't long before Eliza was headed back to Rome, Italy, for her last program review there.

Only the project engineer, Tom, would accompany her this year. He knew Rome well, and they had a friendly relationship. They flew business class into Rome – nothing but the (almost) best for the U.S. Government's underpaid employees. Personally, she would rather have had a raise…. It was her third time in Rome for this tour of duty, but she still thrilled at the sight of the Roman Coliseum as their taxi passed by it on the way to the hotel.

Their first meeting was with the Senior Language Officer (SLO), Nick, at his home, for a family dinner with his wife and two young children. After dinner the three of them went into Nick's study, where they could talk freely behind closed doors. "We'll have our formal talks at the embassy tomorrow," Nick said, "so that several of our cleared personnel can attend conveniently, and stay in the loop. Then on Wednesday I'd like to take you over to the site, for systems checks. Thursday will be a wrap-up and planning session, before you leave on Friday. Agreed?" It would *have* to be – Nick was the boss there.

—

The happy occasion that Eliza's mind dreamed about again and again, while she was lying in her hospital bed in Pennsylvania, was the wedding of the Webers' elder son Georg and his bride Susanne, in the fall of 1999 in Schweinfurt, Germany. Volkmar and Liselotte not only included Eliza and Jon in the festivities, but they invited them to stay at their home for the entire weekend!

It was a day-long event, starting with champagne for the wedding party and family at the Webers' home in the morning. Champagne is always a good idea….

From there, they all drove to the ceremony at the *Rathaus* (town hall), after which there was more champagne and a tiered wedding cake there. Then everyone left for the reception hall to enjoy *Kaffee* and homemade *Kuchen* of all sorts, baked by the female guests. Eventually, everyone went home and had a *Schläfchen* (nap), before going back to the hall for a formal dinner and reception. The evening was marked by free-flowing wine and beer, music and dancing.

At one point, the groomsmen in black masks "kidnapped" the bride, and held her for ransom until the groom was able to pass certain tests required by his friends. All ended well, and the groom received a kiss from his bride for having saved her. It was fascinating for Eliza and Jon to witness a typical Franconian wedding in Bavaria, although the older folks didn't last as long at the reception as did the bridal couple and their friends. That part was the same the world over.

———

Hot nights in Athens! Eliza's last program review before she rotated back to the States was in Athens, Greece, in October of 1999. In this instance the SLO was a woman named Elena, who happened to be Greek-American.

Eliza remembered that Elena always plied her visitors with ouzo, and she was looking forward to it. Every time she came to Greece, Eliza couldn't help noticing how different it was from Germany. Not only did the Greek language have an unfamiliar alphabet, that made all the signs look like a bunch of squiggles, but the weather was much warmer.

The sun shone every day in Athens, as opposed to the almost constant rain in Wiesbaden. The Germans tried to tell her that the Rhine River Valley was responsible for the rain, but Eliza believed that the seriousness of the German people was simply being matched by the weather. Greeks were more laid-back than Germans; either the warmer climate influenced *them*, or else they just wouldn't stand for cold and rain! Elena always spent more time and energy on her yearly ETC visitors than any of the other SLOs. It was more than just her job. She really cared about them, and wanted them to have a profitable and enjoyable week.

One night, Eliza wrote a long string of phrases in her journal that expressed her impressions of Athens, and of Greece itself: waterfalls and ruins, cobblestones and pelicans, Mediterranean food, white-washed houses with blue shutters, mountainous terrain, balconies and narrow streets, hole-in-the-wall bazaars piled high with merchandise from floor to ceiling, stone bridges and laundry hung from balcony to balcony across side streets, pigeons monopolizing town squares, outdoor cafés, wide avenues, and blue skies.

Quite simply, Eliza loved Greece and its people. She wasn't sure that she herself was easygoing enough to live there, but perhaps the beautiful weather would work its magic on *her* personality, too. Not that she would have a chance to test her theory. She had to return to Germany at the end of the week, and in six months she would be on her way back to Maryland. The meetings in Athens were going pretty much as planned, but then Jon arrived on the scene riding his motorcycle!

He had ridden from Wiesbaden, halfway down through the boot of Italy, taken his bike on the ferry over to Greece, and ridden the rest of the way to Athens. He memorized the configuration of Greek squiggles that spelled "Athens," and looked for those squiggles on every road sign he encountered. Somehow he made it to Eliza's hotel and surprised her. He couldn't attend the classified meetings, of course, but Elena welcomed him with open arms and he became an unofficial member of the group.

Now Elena had a surprise of her own. Embassy personnel were being offered a cut-rate weekend cruise of some of the Greek islands, leaving from Athens. Elena cajoled the U.S. Ambassador into allowing her little group of travelers, including Jon, to participate in the cruise. At the ridiculously low cost of only $170 each for two nights, all their meals and entertainment were included! Embassy employees weren't the only passengers, though.

Tourists of every imaginable nationality populated the rest of the small cruise ship, probably paying much more than they did. Before long, they were approaching their first island – Mykonos….

Six

Elena led her little group ashore on Mykonos, and Eliza began to notice the rocky terrain that looked like granite deposits. Numerous beaches dotted the coastline, and some of the tourists were braving the wind to swim or sunbathe. The air felt chilly to her, and she stopped to buy a striped, Greek sailor-style sweater from a vendor along the way. Elena explained that Mykonos was called "island of the winds," because of its strong northern blasts. It had many windmills, that had been used years ago to mill flour.

As they passed through the narrow streets of Mykonos, there were a lot of pelicans walking around. Elena called them their mascots. After lunch on the ship, they stopped again at Patmos, a small island off the west coast of Turkey. There was an air of quiet tranquility there, probably due to the fact that it was mostly Christian pilgrims who visited the island.

Elena took them to the Cave of the Apocalypse, where St. John was said to have received his revelation in a vision of Jesus. John had then dictated to his scribe what was to become the Bible's Book of Revelation.

The last stop of the day was the island of Rhodes, which is at the crossroads between Europe, the Middle East, and Africa. The medieval city of Rhodes had been the site of the Colossus, one of the original Seven Wonders of the World. Evidently the statue of Colossus had towered over the harbor entrance, until it was toppled by a strong earthquake in 226 B.C. Now two bronze deer stand atop their columns, one on each side of the harbor's entry to the city.

"The ship will dock tonight," Elena told them, "and continue on its route back to Athens tomorrow. On the way back, we will stop at a Turkish port for sightseeing and shopping." After dinner on the ship, accompanied by ouzo and champagne, the band began to play a traditional Greek circle dance and Eliza drew Jon out onto the floor. It was actually quite an easy, repetitive step, especially after numerous drinks – on Eliza's part, at least.

The next morning the cruise ship put in at the Turkish port of Kuşadasi, and then the passengers went by bus to Ephesus, twenty kilometers inland. Elena told her little group that Ephesus contained the largest collection of Roman ruins in the Eastern Mediterranean.

They walked along wide, cracked-stone pavement, lined with endless ruins of columns and houses. There were overgrown fields of enormous toppled stones – broken pieces of bas-relief statues of ancient men and women, and drawings and imprints of bare feet. It looked like a forgotten gladiator graveyard, or the result of some monumental earthquake long ago.

The bus took them back to Kuşadasi, where their ship awaited. But before boarding, Elena wanted them to see the carpet-looming process. They watched the women looming, their fingers flying over the colorful threads. Eliza and Jon looked at many carpet runners, but finally settled on a bright red one, with wedding knots fastening the tassels on both ends. Elena closed the deal for them, and asked a crew member she saw on the street to deliver the carpet to their cabin onboard the ship. Soon they were back in Athens, and preparing to return to Wiesbaden.

But what about their Turkish carpet? Jon wouldn't have room for it on his motorcycle, and Eliza would be flying back. It was bulky, and heavy! Elena had the perfect solution…. While Eliza attended the closing remarks for the program review in a classified area of the U.S. Embassy, Elena took Jon down to the shipping department. Together they boxed up the carpet and sent it on its way back to Wiesbaden, courtesy of the U.S. Embassy in Athens.

Only Elena could have managed it so smoothly, and she did it without bothering to ask anyone's permission. Nobody would dare question Elena, and she knew it.

—

Eliza and Jon had tried to celebrate their first Thanksgiving away from home by taking Jon's visiting sister and nephew for a traditional *Ritteressen* (knight's meal) at the *Schloßhotel Rothenbuch* in Germany. It was served at long tables, by candlelight. The only implement provided was what looked like a hunting knife, for spearing and eating whatever was on your plate. Mead was drunk out of pottery mugs, with no handles. Troubadours circulated in period attire, and sang ballads as they played on various instruments of the Middle Ages. It was all very civilized, which was probably one of the non-authentic aspects of the whole experience.

They missed having their traditional American Thanksgiving dinner that year. Consequently, their next two Thanksgivings were spent eating turkey and all the trimmings, but in quite a nontraditional location – the Swiss Alps! The European Technical Center (ETC) put together a pot-luck turkey dinner every Thanksgiving, and everyone drove to Grindelwald, Switzerland, to enjoy it. They took over the whole *Chalet Abendrot* for their accommodations, and enjoyed the town's *Weihnachtsmarkt* (Christmas Market).

Eliza's younger son Chris and his wife joined them for their last Thanksgiving there, in 1999. Skiers were in their element, and cheese fondue was offered at every restaurant. A special railway took them up the famous *Jungfraujoch* Mountain, that seemed as close to heaven as humanly possible. Angela couldn't help entering into this particular dream world of Eliza's, although in disguise this time. It was the happiest she had ever seen her protégée, and it made Angela sad to know that Eliza's life would eventually be hanging in the balance back in Pennsylvania.

Christmas 1999 provided another dream-worthy occasion for Eliza, this time welcoming her older son to Germany. Pete and his girlfriend flew over from Maryland to spend the holiday in Wiesbaden. They all went to the *Weihnachtsmarkt* in Mainz, across the river from Wiesbaden. As everywhere else in Germany, it was an outdoor festival starting in November already – just as Oktoberfest always started in September! They drank hot *Glühwein* (mulled wine) to keep warm, and saved the brightly-colored mugs as souvenirs. When their last Christmas in Germany was just another precious memory, including a visit to *Rothenburg o.d. Taube*, there was still a once-in-a-lifetime event to be celebrated – the fast-approaching millennium!

—

Où allons-nous? À la Tunisie! Where are we going? To Tunisia!

Eliza's favorite overseas country to visit, both professionally and personally, was Tunisia. It was exotic and yet familiar, since it was French-speaking. Tunisia became a French protectorate in 1881, and an independent state in 1956. It was now considered the most competitive economy in Africa, and their women's rights were unmatched by those in any other Arab nation. Jon had come along on her orientation visit there in September of 1997, and they were treated royally in the cosmopolitan capital city, Tunis.

They had shopped in the *souk* (marketplace), and their escort protected them from being bombarded by every vendor that they passed, and from being overcharged when they wanted to buy something. Everyone thought that all American tourists had loads of money. No one would believe that Eliza was just a lowly civil servant. One of the highlights of that first visit to Tunisia was their field trip south to El Jem, to see its spectacular Roman Coliseum. It was built in the third century, by one of the brothers of the Roman dude who built the coliseum in Rome itself.

Its distinction is that the coliseum in Tunisia is the best-preserved of all those built in the Roman Empire. They walked through the underground cells where the gladiators were kept until it was time for their event. It was like being transported back in time, except for the hundreds of feral cats who now roamed the amphitheater's nooks and crannies. Since Eliza had already seen the Roman Coliseum, the difference was obvious – but both were impressive, and the stuff of dreams.

Their host in Tunisia was Ridha, a man whose heart outshone his everyman appearance. On one of Eliza's official trips to his country, she arrived with a seriously-sprained ankle – the worst her German doctor had ever seen. Her leg sported a large, cumbersome brace, and Jon lent her the cane he had used after his knee operation in Germany. Not wanting to draw attention, however, she tried to melt into the crowd that met her plane at the airport in Tunis. No such luck….

Ridha was there to meet her, in the middle of his already crazy day preparing to host various delegations to the yearly conference. She knew that he was more than just her contact in Tunis. He was someone who cared about her – as he cared about his wife, his two little boys, his job, and his country. There was room in his heart for all of them. She was never alone during that week.

While Ridha played tour guide to her colleagues, leading them like the Pied Piper over sand dunes and through their famous coliseum, his right-hand man, Bashir, stayed by her side, offering his arm when they came to steps and sitting with her when she couldn't walk anymore. She never felt pitied or left out of the planned activities. Ridha made sure that the tour ended up wherever she happened to be, with tales of their adventures.

"Were you just trying to get out of coming down here to Tunisia?" Bashir smiled at Eliza, as they had slowly walked through the small airport together.

"You know me better than that," she smiled, too. "Besides, where else would I have the chance to stay in a 5-star hotel, free of charge?"

"Well, we have to treat you right, so you won't pull the rug out from under us," he laughed. Bashir collected all their government passports, and the customs official stamped them automatically – no questions asked. Bashir's day job was as a high-ranking police official. It helped to speed things up. Their van was waiting just outside the door, and the sudden African heat made them appreciate the air-conditioned vehicle they stepped into.

When they arrived at the Abou Nawas Hotel, Bashir got out first and extended his hand to her. She could get used to this! The huge lobby encompassed the entire main floor of the high-rise hotel. It was laid out like a gigantic living room, with armchairs and couches. Bashir collected their passports again and went to check them all in, while they lounged and people-watched.

Hostesses circulated with refreshing fruit drinks while they waited. Eliza couldn't tell if they were spiked or not, but given that Tunisia was a Muslim country, probably not. Bashir was back in no time with their passports, and they were shown to their individual rooms – each one the size of a suite. Bashir brought in her bags from the hall porter. "Just relax, Eliza, and I will help you all I can. Shall I order you something to eat?"

“Only if you stay and join me.”

“I would be honored, Eliza. Thank you.”

Seven

Bashir ordered swordfish steak for their lunch, followed by the traditional hot mint tea. They sat together around the coffee table in the lounging area of Eliza's suite, and he talked about Tunisia as they ate. She could tell that he loved his country very much. "Did you know that Tunis has been called the Paris of North Africa?" Bashir asked her.

"No, but I'm not surprised. Both are very beautiful."

"Why are you so quiet now, Eliza? Is something wrong?"

"It's just that sometimes I feel like I'm locked in a kind of nightmare, and I can't get out – like when my father died while I was in Belgium, and I couldn't save him; or now, hobbling around with a sprained ankle, just from tripping at Lake Como in Italy.

"I wish I could turn back the clock, and maybe things would turn out differently somehow," she said.

"If you figure out how to do that, Eliza, let me know. Everyone has things in their lives that they'd like to change."

"I know you're right, Bashir. My brother called me when our father was admitted to the hospital with pneumonia, at the age of ninety-four. The doctors wanted to know if they should continue to feed him intravenously, given his advanced age. I said yes, of course, even though it only allowed him to live for a while longer. I really wouldn't want to be kept alive by artificial means, if my condition were beyond hope. Would you?"

"Certainly not – but you're not going to die from a sprained ankle, Eliza! I guarantee it, in fact. So I want you to rest for a while before dinner. Your group has been invited to the home of the program director and his wife, here in Tunis."

—

They all assembled in the hotel lobby at the prescribed time, and Bashir was in charge of getting everyone to his boss's house for dinner. Mr. and Mrs. Assid's home was in the suburbs, as befitted his station. They were all greeted with smiles, and plenty of traditional Tunisian food and drink.

The U.S. representatives were always treated well, Eliza noted, because it was American cooperation and money that made their joint projects even possible.

By the time the honey-drenched dessert pastries and mint tea were served, with a sprig of fresh mint in each glass mug, stomachs were bulging and buttons were about to pop off of shirts. "I couldn't even *look* at another pastry!" one guy on Eliza's team exclaimed, as Mr. Assid held out the platter to him again. "They were delicious, though!" he hastened to add.

Mr. Assid disappeared into a side room, and returned with a small pistol in his hand. Pointing it at the guy who had declined seconds, Assid proclaimed, smiling, "You…must…eat!" This being the guy's first program review in Tunisia, he immediately grabbed two of the small pastries from the platter, and shoved them into his mouth. Everyone laughed heartily, although *he* couldn't see anything funny about being threatened with a gun.

The evening ended on an amicable note, as always, but Eliza's hotel room felt very quiet and empty when she returned. The next day, the group took to the road to see some more of the country. They headed south to Hammamet, a walled city on the eastern coast. Then the van continued down the coast, passing through Sousse, another lovely beach resort and sea fortification.

Their final destination for the day was the island of Djerba, off the southeast coast of Tunisia. They were staying overnight at another 5-star resort, the Abou Nawas Golf Hotel. No expense had been spared for Eliza and her team. It was rumored that Libyan leader Muammar Qadafi was vacationing nearby with his entourage, but it couldn't be confirmed. Not that anyone tried. That was one bad dude, and it was best to leave him alone. No one wanted to show up on *his* radar, for any reason. The ETC group went to the Sultan Restaurant for dinner. The big attraction, other than the food, was a bevy of belly dancers hired to entertain the diners.

Those in their group not forbidden by their Muslim religion to drink alcohol enjoyed one carafe after another of the local wine, as they watched the dancers gyrate to the music. These were not middle-aged women with excess belly fat, but instead slim young women who could have been some the men's daughters. When it became apparent that everyone at their table was no longer feeling any pain – excluding the Tunisians, of course – several of the dancers approached them.

They held out their hands to the male members of the team, to invite them to dance. Eliza was safe, being the only female guest and sporting an ankle brace besides. None of the guys were allowed to say no, however, and soon the dance floor was filled with undulating couples, some making absolute spectacles of themselves.

After they all had a few more drinks, Bashir drove them back to the hotel and they were grateful to have a designated driver. They agreed on a time to leave in the morning, and dispersed to their rooms.

They all headed back to the mainland in the van the next morning, with a stop to check on their project's construction. The rest of the trip was devoted to sightseeing, with the primary destination being Matmata. Ridha knew that Americans were always interested in seeing the desert locations where their *Star Wars* films were made, including the caves where the troglodytes had once lived. They were a prehistoric race of cavemen in North Africa. Today, the term troglodyte has come to mean anyone who prefers the life of a hermit, with no interest in modern technology.

—

Fast forward to Eliza's son Pete's Christmas visit to Germany with his girlfriend in 1999. They planned to stay through New Year's – into the new millennium! After seeing the desert set of *Star Wars* herself, Eliza just knew that was exactly where she wanted to take them during their visit. "Yippee! We're all going to Tunisia!" she surprised them, at Christmastime in Wiesbaden. Ridha was their tour guide once more, on a two-day desert safari that started with Matmata and the Coliseum at El Jem.

Then farther south to Douz, where they all had the opportunity to ride one-humped dromedaries – not to be confused with ordinary camels, they were told. These domesticated animals can be over six feet tall! Eliza had heard that the dromedaries liked to bite when they were impatient, so she was glad they had been muzzled. Everyone was exhausted after traipsing through the sand, and swaying back and forth on pseudo-camels' backs! They stayed overnight in Douz, at the aptly-named Hotel Sahara, but the accommodations were rather rustic – more like cots in barracks. They were too tired to care….

Eliza thought that the great salt lake at Chott El Djerid the next day would resemble the one in Utah, and that she could take a refreshing dip. No such luck. It was almost dry, due to the oncoming summer's heat, and only good for wetting one's feet. Even that felt good, though. That night they stopped close to the Algerian border at the Oasis of Tozeur, near the great salt lake. Many thousands of palm trees were thriving there, and their luscious dates were plentiful. Cascading waterfalls made you forget where you were – in the desert!

Back at the 4-star Hammamet Garden Hotel, the four of them kicked back and relaxed at the pool, getting mentally ready for the New Year's Eve Millennium celebration at the hotel. They all dressed up for the occasion, and enjoyed the gala dinner buffet and entertainment. Their young male server jokingly offered Pete several camels for his blond girlfriend, but she was not for sale at any price!

After midnight, on January 1st, 2000, Pete privately proposed to her, with the Spangenberg-family antique opal-and-diamond ring. She said yes, but their happiness was relatively short-lived as time went on, and they never married.

Eliza wanted to believe that such heartbreak served a purpose in all of their lives. Otherwise, how would any of them survive…?

—

Not to be outdone that spring, Eliza's younger son Chris graduated with honors from Longwood Gardens Professional Gardener Training Program in Pennsylvania. She and Jon flew home for the occasion, of course, and it felt to her like one of those dream sequences, where everything goes beautifully. Chris won two of the four awards given in the course of the evening: The Director's Award for scholarship, work performance, and leadership; and the Academic Achievement Award for the highest cumulative grade-point average (4.0)!

A few weeks after returning to ETC, its Director invited Ridha and the SLO in Tunis to attend project updates in Wiesbaden. Ridha had filled his suitcases with everything needed to make the whole ETC Tunisia team a special couscous lunch, including raw lamb! He had packed it in dry ice, in a checked bag at the airport, and no one was the wiser. He must have lied through his teeth about what he was bringing into Germany! Luckily, it was a short flight!

He was an excellent cook, and he used every pot and burner in ETC's little kitchenette to bring his masterpiece to fruition. The tray of juicy braised lamb alone was enough to make the rest of ETC salivate, as it was carried down the hall for the feast. Seasoned to perfection, the couscous mixed with fresh vegetables from a Wiesbaden market tempted even the most conservative of American palates. The only thing lacking was a bottle of local wine, which of course was not allowed on U.S. government property. Ridha didn't even miss it, though.

The cooperation between the U.S. and Tunisia would go on even after Eliza left Germany, she was sure, but there would be a hole in her heart where Ridha and Bashir had once been. The big boss of the Tunisian end of the joint project, Mr. Assid, was also a very kind-hearted man. When he and his wife celebrated the wedding of their son, Mohamed, before Eliza and Jon rotated back to the States, Eliza sent them a congratulatory card that read:

They climbed the clouds,
They rode the skies,
A look of wonder in their eyes.
And each one knew this day would be
Forever shared in memory.
May love's happy journey take you
To the most wonderful places!

Best wishes to your whole family, and I hope we will have the opportunity to see you again soon.
Regards, Eliza and Jon Layton

Eight

Angela was glad to see Eliza and Jon whenever they returned to Wiesbaden from their travels. She could always whisk off in spirit occasionally, to invisibly check on Eliza's well-being, but God would let her know if there were an urgent need for her guardianship. Otherwise, Angela was busy maintaining her cover as a liaison officer herself, and the travel that entailed, until they all rotated back to the States. Right now it was more important for Eliza to keep dreaming positive dreams about her travels in Europe with Jon, to help bring her safely out of her COVID-induced coma in Pennsylvania.

Maybe it was time for Angela to have a talk with Jon, without divulging her role as Eliza's guardian angel. He should be made aware of how crucial he would be in helping to save his wife's life in the future. Why should he believe her, though? That was the question....

"Hey, Jon. It's Angela at ETC. I guess Eliza told you that Ridha was here for talks, and that he was cooking lunch for the whole Tunisia team today. Neither of us is included, however, and I was wondering if you'd be free to meet me for lunch in town. There's something I want to talk to you about – concerning Eliza."

"She's not in trouble with the boss, is she?" he laughed.

"No, nothing like that. Is there a place near your house where I could meet you for a quick lunch, and then get back to work?"

"Sure. There's a Greek sandwich place on *Föhrer Straße*, three blocks from our house. What time?"

"I know the one you mean – how about noon?"

"I'll be there."

"Thanks, Jon."

Jon was waiting at a patio table when Angela showed up, already sipping a coke. He was almost sixty by now, and Angela looked like she could have been his daughter – quite a common sight in Europe. The Greek owner appeared with two complimentary glasses of ouzo, which Jon declined.

The owner served Angela and sat down at their table himself, shaking his head. Not wanting to waste the other ouzo, he clinked glasses with Angela and they each did a quick down-the-hatch. Then he sent over the waiter to take their order, and disappeared into the café.

Once they were alone and she'd had a drink, Angela felt a bit more confident to tackle the subject at hand. "I'm very fond of your wife, Jon," she began.

"I know, and she's lucky to have your friendship." *Where the heck is this going?*

"I'm something of a clairvoyant, I guess you might say, and I see something in the distant future that I want to warn you about – as it pertains to Eliza."

"Go on…."

"In twenty years, there will be a global pandemic of the coronavirus, dubbed COVID-19, that will sicken and even kill millions of people the world over. Eliza will eventually be affected by one of its many variants, and hospitalized. She will lapse into a coma, and at that time I will be the nurse assigned to take care of her. You and I will work together to try and save her, but we may not be successful. Your job is to fill her life with happy memories of your travels together now. These memories will be the basis of her dreams, while her body is trying to recuperate.

"We want to give her the will to go on living then, if we can, without worrying her about it now, however," Angela concluded.

"That's a lot to take in, but I'll do everything I can to provide her with lots of good memories. How do you know if your predictions are accurate, though?"

"All I can say is that I have it on good authority that my prophecy is trustworthy, Jon."

"You mean, like a crystal ball?"

"Something like that, only better…."

Jon was skeptical as he walked back home, after Angela had made such an ominous prediction of a world health crisis that would affect Eliza personally – and their life together, too. Where would they even be living by that time? But according to Angela, at least both of them *would* still be alive! That was a revelation in itself – he would be eighty by then, and Eliza in her mid-seventies! One thing was for certain, though. There was no way he would burden her with Angela's disclosure – it would be hard enough for *him* to live with that knowledge….

—

But it was only the year 2000 now, and Eliza had another four months to go as a liaison officer in Wiesbaden.

When their German friends, the Webers, proposed a final joint trip to Berlin, Eliza and Jon jumped at the chance – to see them, and Berlin, again. Actually, for Jon it would be his first time there, although Eliza had spent some months in Berlin on temporary duty (TDY) ten years ago. Volkmar filled them in on his childhood memories of a Berlin under Communism, while Liselotte was anticipating the opportunity to go shopping there with Eliza.

First came sightseeing – Jon's initial sights and sounds of the vibrant capital: the Brandenburg Gate, *Unter den Linden* Avenue, the *Reichstag* (Parliament), Checkpoint Charlie Museum, *Kurfürstendamm* Avenue, remnants of the Berlin Wall, and *Alexanderplatz* with its view of the stately Television Tower from their Forum-Hotel-Berlin skyscraper. Unfortunately, no photos were taken – they were too busy sightseeing! They were all impressed with the extensive renovations to the former East Berlin, of course.

Liselotte and Eliza left Jon in the capable hands of his tour guide, Volkmar, while they headed for the department stores on *Kurfürstendamm*. "Look at this lovely beige-leather jacket, Eliza," Liselotte said, trying it on. "Volkmar will say that I have enough jackets and coats – but nothing like this, from Berlin! And it's not too expensive, either."

"It looks great on you, Liselotte. You should get it. I wish I could find something, too…. Let's try another store."

They wandered into a French department store, of all things, and there was the perfect rain jacket for Eliza – and it was reversible, too – black on one side and cream-colored on the other. The fabric had a sheen to it, and it was a very stylish three-quarter length. "You could wear that for any occasion, Eliza – casual or dressy. And God knows we get our share of rain in Germany!" Eliza took her friend's advice, and they both changed into their new jackets and put the old ones into their store bags. They surprised their husbands later, who barely recognized them when they all met up for lunch!

—

The clock was ticking ever closer to the end of their PCS, and Easter was approaching. Eliza and Jon had developed a friendship with her newfound cousin Gudrun and husband Tom, and they were invited to visit them at their home in Nienhagen for the occasion. Gudrun's great-great-grandfather and Eliza's great-grandfather were half-brothers. Gudrun's ancestor had stayed in Nienhagen, Germany, while Eliza's came to the U.S. and settled in Erie, Pennsylvania. Gudrun's husband Tom built their house himself on the outskirts of the small village, and it overlooked the German countryside.

The former horse barn on the property had been converted into a study for Tom, with a guest bedroom upstairs. That was where Jon and Eliza slept, under the eaves.

A precarious ladder-style spiral staircase led down to the first-floor bathroom, however, discouraging midnight potty runs. Staying with them was a gourmet's delight. Breakfast consisted of endless cups of good, strong German coffee, fresh *brötchen* (hard rolls), plates brimming with various cheeses and cold cuts, *Müesli* (granola cereal) and yogurt, homemade jams and local honey.

After some area sightseeing, they all returned home and Gudrun insisted on fixing dinner. It was her famous salmon bake, for ten people – their daughter and family, who lived upstairs from them, were included, as well as Gudrun's brother and family! It consisted of salmon filets, fresh *Spargel* (white asparagus), boiled parsley potatoes, a whole head of steamed cauliflower ringed with fresh-cooked peas and carrots, and for dessert – vanilla ice cream with a pistachio sauce. The wine and beer flowed like water, and it wasn't over until 10 PM!

—

When the time came to return to the States for good, Eliza sometimes pondered their three years in Germany from the standpoint of pedestrian-and-traffic regulations, of all things! In Germany, rules were made to be followed, which is what Germans do best. Jay-walking is against the law there, and that law is actually enforced. Eliza never saw anyone jay-walk during the entire time she and Jon lived in Germany.

What they did see were pedestrians waiting to cross the street at an intersection – and waiting, and waiting…for the little walking-man on the sign to light up. No one would even think to cross when the red hand was lit up. It didn't matter if there were not a single car in sight in any direction. Germans will wait forever for the permission to cross. Eliza and Jon's tendency was to cross anyway, but the looks they got from other pedestrians discouraged them in no time at all.

Officials tried to institute a right-turn-after-stop regulation in some German cities, but no one took advantage of it – so they removed the signs. Stopping and waiting at a red light was just too completely ingrained in their collective psyche for that.   They do have an interesting rule about intersections, however, many of which have no traffic lights or stop signs – no signs of any kind! If two vehicles approach such an intersection at the same time but from different directions, the car on the right has the undisputed right of way. This is quite orderly, and German, when you stop to think about it.

France is not quite as orderly a country, since individualism reigns supreme there. But their round-abouts have a certain, though odd, flow to them. Cars coming *into* the circle have the right of way. Trying to emerge from the round-about that encircles the *Arc de Triomphe* in Paris, for example, can be an all-day affair.   Such merry-go-rounds have even been immortalized in movies like *European Vacation*.

Since those already *in* the circle have no rights whatsoever, they must wait until no one is trying to come in, before they can get out. That could take a lifetime, in Parisian traffic!

When May of 2000 rolled around, Eliza and Jon, and even Angela, had completed three years of a whirlwind life in Germany. It was the classic American *modus operandi*, of seeing as much as you can in the shortest time possible. Eliza had to admit that her carpe-diem mentality kicked in the minute their plane landed in Frankfurt in 1997, and didn't let her rest until they put a final wheels-down again in Maryland. Many of her memories of that time eventually began to dim, but the feeling of gratitude for the priceless opportunity they had been given remained strong.

Nine

Angela finished her own 3-year tour in Wiesbaden first, and reappeared back in the States to find herself another apartment in Laurel, Maryland. As an angel, she didn't need somewhere to live, but in her human form she needed food and a place to sleep just like everyone else. It was a hassle, but she was devoted to Eliza and her well-being since being appointed by God to be her guardian angel. Eliza would need Angela more and more as her health declined over the years, and especially as her nurse when Eliza contracted COVID and slipped into a coma in 2022.

But for now, Eliza and Jon were back in their townhouse in Laurel, although still waiting for their furniture to arrive from Wiesbaden. They had rented out their empty house for the three years they were gone, and now it needed lots of work.

So they stayed nearby with her son Pete and his fiancée for three weeks, but driving back and forth from their townhouse got old. They decided to just stay in their house full-time, and bought a cheap hide-a-bed futon. But it was too uncomfortable to sleep on at night, so they dragged the thin mattress off the couch at bedtime and laid it out on the carpet. It gave new meaning to the concept of "rolling out of bed in the morning."

Angela was happy to have them back, but she was powerless to protect them from what happened only two weeks after they returned. They were in a car accident on busy Route 1 in Laurel, on a Friday afternoon in rush-hour traffic. Jon was driving their rental pick-up truck, which was handy for picking up such things as hide-a-beds at the warehouse. They were turning left into a shopping center in the middle of the block. The oncoming cars, that were waiting for their light to turn green, parted to let them turn. After Jon looked both ways, a woman driving an SUV must have switched lanes and she came barreling toward them out of nowhere. Witnesses said that she was going at least twice the speed limit, and T-boned their truck on Eliza's side. Glass flew everywhere, but at first Eliza didn't think that she was hurt. Her right elbow was scratched and it hurt a bit, but it wasn't until later that her side started to ache. She went to the emergency room and the x-rays showed that, yes indeed, she had a fracture of the second-last rib. They don't tape you up anymore for that, so they gave her prescriptions for pain pills and anti-inflammatories, and sent her on her way.

They said that it would heal in four to six weeks, but after three weeks she still couldn't roll over in bed or be on her feet for more than half an hour without being totally exhausted. It really slowed her down, during a period when they had so many plans for fixing up their house and traveling. They actually traveled anyway, mainly to visit family and sleep in real beds from time to time. She knew she would survive, but it wasn't much fun at the moment.

Many returnees from Germany made the decision to get out of the Washington, D.C., area. Now that Eliza had seen for herself how crazily people drove around there, she couldn't wait for her time to be up so that they could leave, too. Visiting her son Chris on the Eastern Shore of Maryland convinced her that a quieter, gentler way of life really did exist. They just had to find it for themselves. Eliza started back to work at NSA after two months of paid home-leave. They still felt a bit like misplaced persons in the U.S., but were essentially glad to be back.

—

Angela and Eliza were together in the same office again when they returned to work at NSA Headquarters. It was like old times, although they both missed ETC and living in Germany. Eliza knew that Angela's directive from on high was to stay in close touch with her, but Eliza worried that it was because she was in some kind of danger.

"Sometimes I feel like I'm a kid again, Angela, and you're my babysitter. What are you afraid will happen to me?"

"We guardian angels are charged with being proactive, and warding off trouble if we can. That's not always possible, though, like when another driver caused your truck accident. Let me ask you a question, Eliza. Would you feel more comfortable if I were invisible to you, as most angels are, instead of taking human form as your friend and colleague?"

"No – because then we couldn't talk the way we do, and I couldn't ask you for advice…."

"Isn't that what husbands are for…?"

"Very funny…. I mean as woman to woman."

"Angels don't *have* gender, unless we take human form. We're spiritual beings, despite people's perception of Gabriel or St. Michael the Archangel as male figures. Or God, for that matter…."

"Let's just keep things the way they are, Angela, okay? I've been through enough changes lately to last me a while."

"I understand. Getting used to living back here in the States isn't easy, but change is a part of human life. I can't guarantee you that nothing about your life will ever change, Eliza, for the good or otherwise.

"All I can do is help you to adjust, and try to smooth the way for you if I can."

"That's a lot – and I'm grateful to you. Thank you...."

—

That night, Eliza was trapped yet again in the recurring nightmare that had plagued her ever since their last trip to Berlin with the Webers. Her anxiety over returning to the States always took the form of an ill-fated flight in a small plane, whose young pilot said he had no idea how to take off or land safely. The first time she had this dream was only six weeks before their eventual move back home, after three years in Germany. She was feeling out of control about embarking on that unknown journey – a new office job ahead, and readjustment to living in the U.S. again.

Now she was running into obstacles along the way, like the teenagers in her dream who refused to get out of the path as her plane taxied down the runway. Eliza had been anxious to have a worry-free flight home and an effortless transition, but now she knew it was up to her to make it happen. Not even Angela could live her life for her. Eliza had to take over the controls, and land the plane safely herself.

—

Life went on, including an ordinary day at work in the fall of 2001. That is, until the United States was attacked by terrorists on September 11, and all their lives changed forever. Eliza was in her office on the tenth floor of an 11-floor NSA Headquarters building in Maryland. Suddenly two passenger planes each slammed into one of the two World Trade Center towers in New York City, one after the other – eventually bringing both skyscrapers crashing to the ground, and killing around three thousand people.

The only TV monitor was in the branch chief's office, and it was already blaring. Everyone tried to squeeze into his office to find out what was going on. Obviously the communications their office regularly monitored in the top U.S. spy agency were not as compelling that morning as the live TV coverage of the attack that was taking place before their eyes.

Eliza stood with her colleagues, Angela by her side, watching in horror but not able to move from the spot as the two moments of impact were replayed over and over again. "Did you know this was going to happen, Angela?" Eliza turned to her and whispered, so as not to be overheard.

"No – I'm as shocked as you are, Eliza! God keeps many things regarding the future from *all* of us, I'm afraid."

When it was announced that a third plane had hit the Pentagon in nearby Washington, D.C., something inside Eliza snapped. She pulled Angela out of the branch chief's office, and away from the others who were pushing to get in closer. "We have to get out of here, now!" she told her angelic friend. "We're sitting ducks at the top of a government high-rise building!"

"I agree, Eliza. Lead the way…."

So, as everyone else stood glued to the TV screen, they walked back to their desks, turned off their computers, locked any paperwork in their desks, and calmly strode out of the office. Eliza had paused on the way out to call Jon at home on the black office phone – an outside line as opposed to her personal gray phone, which was a secure line within and between agencies. To save time, all she told him was to turn on the TV and that she was headed home. He had lots of questions, but she had already hung up.

The halls were empty, and no one was waiting for any of the eight elevators on their floor. Eliza pushed the down-button, and one of the doors slid open as though it had been waiting just for them. The only person on the elevator was a young man in uniform, who looked as worried as they were. When they reached the ground floor, there was no one else exiting the building with them! The three parted ways, Angela giving Eliza a hug and asking her to keep in touch. There was no way they'd be required to come back to work until further notice.

The parking lot was a sea of 20,000+ vehicles, but no one appeared to be leaving at the same time they were. It was incomprehensible to Eliza how the entire building could be in such a trance that their flight impulse had been totally disabled. Eliza had German ancestry, but even *she* could assess the danger and take action without corporate permission. She always parked in the same general area and her car was waiting for her, as anxious as she was to be off of government property. She made it home in fifteen minutes, as usual, since the Baltimore-Washington Parkway wasn't crowded in the middle of a normal weekday.

Jon was watching the live coverage on TV, and looked up. "I can't believe this is happening, Eliza! Did they send everyone home?"

"No, Angela and I just decided to leave, before *our* building was turned into a fireball, too! No one else was getting out, though. They were just standing around watching the destruction on TV. It was like they were mesmerized or something!"

"Well, I'm glad you're home. Nobody knows what to expect next...."

As they sat there together and watched both Towers collapse into rubble, they were thankful for each other. Eliza called Angela to make sure she got back to her apartment safely. "Yes, I'm here – just waiting for instructions from God. He might need His angels to join forces in a rescue mission in NYC, or elsewhere.

"This is beginning to resemble Armageddon, Eliza!"

"I just want you to know that you can come and stay with us, if you don't want to be alone, Angela…. "

"Thanks, Eliza. I'm supposed to be looking after *you*, but I know you're in good hands now that you're home. I'll keep you posted about my whereabouts."

Later in the morning it was announced that NSA was evacuating its buildings, and sending everyone home. Eliza was glad that she hadn't waited for the official order, though. She could just imagine the traffic jam, with everyone driving out of the parking lots at once!

Ten

As a precaution after 9-11, all U.S. commercial flights were cancelled for a period of time. The problem was that Jon's elder son and his fiancée were getting married in Taiwan just two weeks later, and Jon and Eliza were planning to attend. The bride and groom had met in the capital of Taipei, where they both worked, so it wasn't necessary for *them* to travel. U.S. planes were flying again by then, but it was risky. On the other hand, Jon didn't want to miss his son's wedding, so they threw caution to the winds and went ahead with their plans.

No problem! Their flight to Los Angeles from Baltimore-Washington International Airport (BWI) was practically empty, since everyone was too afraid to fly. Eliza was actually surprised that the NSA Security Office had given her permission to fly to the Far East, but then that part of the world wasn't perceived to be the source of the current threat.

It wouldn't have prevented terrorists from hijacking their plane, though. Eliza shared with Jon what the Security Office had told her to do in the event of a hijacking. First of all, don't sit in an aisle seat, since terrorists would grab those people first. She was told not to use her official government passport, either, because you wouldn't want a terrorist to know that you worked for the U.S. Defense Department. If the hijackers collected everyone's passports, her regular tourist passport wouldn't single her out as anyone special, much less as someone with inside information. They both tried to keep a low profile, and she told no one who her employer was.

They were just traveling to Taiwan for a family wedding, which was the truth. As per instructions, they carried no pictures of their kids or grandkids in their wallets. Those could be used as leverage against them, in a hostage situation. From Los Angeles, they flew the Taiwanese National Airline, Eva Air, to Taipei. The 747 was packed, but Jon's son had advised them to pay an extra $125 each for "deluxe-tourist" seats, that provided more leg room even if the person in front of you reclined their back-rest. The female flight attendants wore traditional Taiwanese attire and everything onboard was first-rate for 2001, including the food, complimentary slippers, and sleep-masks.

—

Jon's son had also booked their hotel in Taipei, and it was conveniently located near his own apartment.

As they walked the hallways to and from their room, however, it was quite apparent that prostitutes were renting certain rooms by the hour. There was a steady stream of men, all hours of the day and night. Or maybe it was just the hotel whores – available to guests for an additional charge. At least the women were friendly, though, and didn't keep other guests awake at night….

As Jon and Eliza strolled the streets of Taipei in their free time before the day of the wedding, they tried to sample the local culture. Going into a corner sandwich shop, they sat down on stools at the lunch counter. Beside them sat a couple with two young girls who were about five years old, and obviously twins. The parents spoke halting English, which was better than their own nonexistent Chinese. Eliza was always amazed wherever they traveled at how widespread the use of English was, however rudimentary. It was a humbling experience.

"Welcome to Taiwan," the father said. "Americans?"

"Yes," Jon answered. "My son is getting married here."

"His wife Taiwanese?"

"No, she is Chinese, but she was raised in England. They both work here, though."

"Ah...." That must have been confusing to him. "We love America! My daughters have American names – Coke, and Cola."

"Ah...." How could you politely respond to that?

As they continued to stroll after lunch, they passed a jewelry store, and Eliza insisted on going in. She had a tradition of buying a souvenir piece of jewelry on every major trip they took, even if it was only a pair of amber earrings in the Czech Republic or an inexpensive shell ring in Florida when they visited Jon's daughter. She fell in love with a star-sapphire ring in Taipei, that reminded her of the late Princess Diana's engagement ring. It wasn't cheap, however, and Angela stood by her invisibly and whispered a warning in her ear, not to trust the jeweler.

Eliza didn't listen to her angel, of course, and bought the ring anyway. Almost twenty years later, when her son Pete wanted to propose to the new love of his life, he asked her for one of her many rings as an engagement ring. Eliza spread out the contents of her ring container, a porcelain dish with a picture of the Spangenberg Schloß on the top. They sat on her bed, and she told him where she had bought or been given each of the rings.

The one he picked was the star sapphire ring from Taipei, with a crystal starburst surrounding it.

They were fairly sure that Princess Diana's ring would have had a diamond starburst, but he loved this one anyway and she readily gave it to him. The story had a happy ending when his girlfriend said yes to his proposal and also loved the ring, but when they took it to a local jeweler for resizing they found out that it was a fake sapphire! So they had it reset with a smaller sapphire, as well as resized, and both Eliza and Angela were heartbroken. Angela had at least *tried* to warn her those many years ago.

—

The wedding in Taipei in 2001 was like nothing they had ever seen before. The bride wore a long, red-silk sheath, with a mandarin collar and a slit up the side. No one had told Eliza and Jon that red was the traditional color for weddings there, so they had both dressed in beige for late summer. They stuck way out amid all the other guests who had obviously gotten the message. Even the mother of the groom, Jon's ex-wife, was dressed in red. The ceremony was held at the Taipei town hall, and six couples were married by the female judge – all at the same time!

All the couples were Chinese-speaking, except Jon's son and his family, so the judge said everything in both Chinese and English, for their benefit. At least that way the groom knew what he was getting into! The festivities went on that day and into the next, ending with an extravagant brunch the next morning.

Eliza wore a long, brightly-flowered sheath, which would have been a more appropriate color for the wedding, but how was an American to know these things without a heads-up? The bridal couple then left for their honeymoon in Bali, leaving Eliza and Jon to their next big adventure before flying home – a group tour of Beijing!

Their plane stopped over in Hong Kong, before continuing to Beijing, and they exchanged some currency at the airport. Unfortunately, now they had Hong Kong dollars, which were not accepted on the Chinese mainland! Just another American faux pas to add to the list. *Americans don't get out much, do they?* But there was more excitement to come…. They were the only English-speaking members of the tour group, the others being Taiwanese, so they couldn't take the same tour bus once they all landed in Beijing!

They were assigned to a private car, with their own male driver and female tour guide – or as Jon like to think of them – driver-spy and tour-guide-spy. The two spies spoke Chinese to each other, but English to them. Jon had the feeling that they were keeping tabs on the Americans because of Eliza's job, but how would they have known where she worked…? *How indeed?* When they settled into their hotel room, Jon started looking for listening devices but he wasn't James Bond, after all. *Angela* probably knew if they were being spied on, but she wasn't telling. Even so, they watched what they said to each other.

The sights they were shown included places they never thought they would see in their lifetime – the Forbidden City, Tian'anmen Square, the Summer Palace, and the Great Wall of China, outside the city. When John got his photos developed in Taipei later, he had them transferred to a CD before they flew back home to Maryland. Because of 9-11, he was afraid that the exposed film would be damaged when it went through the intensified U.S. airport scanners of carry-on luggage. One of the first things they did after they unpacked their suitcases at home was to access the CD on Jon's computer.

"You won't believe this, Eliza! Come and look at our pictures from the wedding and of mainland China…."

"Looks like we got some good ones of the wedding festivities – but wait, what's that blank space?"

"That's where our four pictures of Tian'anmen Square would have been. They were deleted…!"

"You mean censored?"

"That's exactly what I mean. They were probably considered too political, after that huge massacre of student protesters there in 1989…!"

—

Eliza's job at the National Security Agency soon changed drastically, since the Agency's new focus after 9-11 became the capture of Osama Bin Laden. Everyone who worked there was faced with the possibility of being transferred to crisis cells, and of doing shift work. It was now an agency-wide 24/7 operation, even in the foreign-language offices, and French or German were not the language proficiencies that were most needed. Linguists who could read and understand Arabic and its dialects were in demand, but many of them were not U.S. citizens and therefore they could not be granted the necessary top-secret security clearances – or any clearances, for that matter.

Eliza was approaching twenty years of government service and she met the other requirements for the early-retirement package being offered at that time. It included a $25K incentive and full retirement benefits, and seemed like an easy decision to make. She reached the twenty-year mark on the very last day of the early-retirement-window deadline, and submitted her paperwork. It was time for a change of pace, and Eliza retired in January of 2002, at the age of 57. Her guardian angel was less than pleased….

"Couldn't we have done another overseas tour before you threw in the towel, Eliza? *London* would have been nice!" Angela knew that she would have no reason to stay at NSA after Eliza left, although she could always become invisible again.

"Yes, it would be nice…and there are some open three-year tours in Hawaii, and Australia, too. But Jon thinks it would be boring to ride a motorcycle around a small Hawaiian island, and the thought of snakes and scorpions in Australia's Outback would give me nightmares!"

"What about London, then? They speak English there!" *The last thing Eliza needs is to remember more nightmares!*

"There's just one problem – I don't have a high enough grade level for the job. My boss would probably snatch it out from under my nose, anyway."

"So, what's the plan, now that you're officially retired?"

"How would you feel about North Carolina? The weather is bound to be warmer than Maryland, and besides – who said anything about retiring for good…?"

Eleven

Eliza had lived in Maryland for over thirty years, much longer than she had lived anywhere else, including growing up in Erie, Pennsylvania. But now she and Jon were looking for a place that was more relaxed than the hectic pace of the Baltimore/Washington corridor, somewhere less expensive, and somewhere warmer. After looking around the country for years at different retirement locations, they kept returning to the idea of Asheville, North Carolina, in the aftermath of 9-11. It was far enough from the Washington area to make them a little less nervous….

So, even before Eliza officially retired from NSA, they headed to Asheville again for a long weekend in November – Veterans' Day, which was a three-day weekend for government employees and also happened to include Eliza's birthday.

It was a town that kept drawing them back, and this time they decided to look at the real-estate magazines when they stopped for lunch. There it was – the drawing of a house that was under construction, just west of Asheville. They met the realtor there the next day, and loved it immediately.

The view of the valley itself was enough for Eliza, but the house was a dream – a modified A-frame façade, a large front deck, and a master-bedroom suite forming a private loft upstairs. Finding that house made her decision to retire even easier, and all the pieces seemed to be falling into place. They bought the house and moved down in March, before Easter. When they adopted a four-month-old golden-retriever-mix puppy named Autumn soon after that, their little local family was complete. She became their grand-dog and the *Land of the Sky*, as Asheville was called, became their new home.

Jon began working part-time at the Biltmore Estate Winery, and Eliza started teaching French part-time at Western Carolina University. Having a new mortgage to pay had put their dreams of a complete retirement on hold. When the school year was over, however, Eliza looked for a summer job while Jon continued at the Biltmore Estate. She found it at the Biltmore's rival tourist destination in Asheville, the Grove Park Inn Resort Hotel and Spa. It seemed that Mr. Vanderbilt had been a contemporary of Mr. Grove's.

The two had agreed to keep out of each other's way – Grove building his resort in northern Asheville, and Vanderbilt placing the largest privately-owned home in America on a huge estate in southern Asheville.

Both undertakings were completed in the early 1900s, and the Grove Park Inn was a masterpiece of local stonework with a world-class indoor/outdoor pool and spa. Eliza underwent an extensive orientation there, and then began working as a hostess in their open-air terrace dining room, overlooking the Blue Ridge Mountains. The view alone was worth the price of dining there, and many celebrities enjoyed lunch on the terrace during her early shift that summer. Some left extravagant tips, even for her!

—

God thought it best for Angela to withdraw her human presence from Eliza's life for a while, when they moved to North Carolina. She would still maintain an invisible presence, as most guardian angels did, and the two of them could share their thoughts with each other as needed. Eliza would probably not be happy with this decision, however.

"Have you always been with me invisibly as my guardian angel, Angela?"

"Always…ever since you were born, Eliza. It's my assignment to help you whenever I can, and I will continue to do so.

"There have been times when you needed guidance," Angela said, "like during your divorce from your first husband. I was there to comfort you, even though you didn't know me then."

"But now that we've become friends, too, I'll really miss seeing you, Angela…."

"I know… me, too, but I'll still be with you, and we can share our thoughts as much as you want." Angela gave Eliza a final hug, and disappeared from her sight. Eliza couldn't even tell Jon about it, since he only knew Angela as a colleague and friend of his wife.

—

Now in 2022, it was time for Angela to start promoting Eliza's happy dreams, however, especially the ones that hadn't involved Jon. As soon as Eliza went to sleep that night, Angela reminded her subconsciously of a trip she had taken in 1988 with her son Chris, who was only seventeen years old at the time. He was just about to graduate from high school, and she was living alone then except for him and their cocker spaniel, Taffy. Her graduation present to Chris was to be a trip for the two of them to France, over Easter break. He had been studying French, but had never been overseas.

They flew into Paris and did the tourist thing together, even though Eliza had been there several times, once as a chaperone for her high school French students.

She loved seeing Paris through his eyes, and they even planned to go to the Moulin Rouge Cabaret revue one evening. She couldn't believe that they actually denied her son entry into the show, however, because he wasn't quite eighteen yet! Who would have thought that the French would be such sticklers about age, or that the topless revue would contain anything he hadn't already seen somewhere?

Oh well.… They rented a car and hit the road driving west, toward the Atlantic coast. Unfortunately, when they stopped for gas they realized that their car was designed to take only unleaded fuel, which wasn't yet available at every gas station in the country. It was 1988, and only about a dozen gas stations scattered throughout France even had it! The attendant gave them a map of France that pinpointed the stations that offered unleaded gas, and they had to plan their route around its availability! The upside was that they got to see parts of northern France that they hadn't planned to visit.…

When they reached the west coast and glimpsed the island of Mont St. Michel and the beach resort of St. Malo, Eliza remembered her trip to France with her students about eight years ago – how a senior girl around Chris's age right now got lost in the Louvre Museum at closing time! Eliza was tasked with finding her, since she herself was the newest faculty member among the chaperones. Then this same adventurous girl sneaked out after the bed-check in St. Malo, and spent the whole night carousing with the male soccer team from Denmark, on the beach no less!

They found her alone and asleep on the beach the next morning, and wondered what to tell her parents – if she turned out to be pregnant. Fortunately, that hadn't happened, but they didn't let her out of their sight for the rest of the bus trip back to Paris. Eliza began to wish that she and Chris had taken a bus tour instead of using a rental car, by the time *they* got back to Paris for their flight home. Finding gas stations with unleaded fuel was a hassle, and more expensive, too.

———

Maybe having Eliza remember *those* trips wasn't the completely happy dreamland experience that Angela was hoping for, the angel realized. But there had been another mother-son trip, sixteen years later, that might provide a more satisfying memory for Eliza to draw upon in her hospital plight. In 2004, her older son Pete had mentioned that he had an unused plane ticket for a flight from Honolulu to Fiji, because he had cancelled out on the professional conference he was supposed to attend there.

He said that he had to use the ticket before summer, to go somewhere that Hawaiian Airlines flew. When Eliza asked him what his choices were, all she heard in the list was TAHITI, and she knew that they were destined to go there together! It was a French-speaking island paradise that she had always wanted to visit! Eliza, at 60, was on Spring Break from teaching in North Carolina, and Pete, at 35, took time off from his doctoral program at the University of Maryland.

They landed in the capital of Tahiti, Pape'ete, after thirty-three hours on four different flights! After crashing overnight – at the hotel, that is – they visited the old marketplace and the cathedral, which was the only building in Pape'ete that wasn't destroyed by the Germans in WWI. Then they took a ferry to another island, Mo'orea, where they stayed the rest of the week, sleeping in a cozy grass hut on the beach. They each had their own little bed equipped with a mosquito net, and there was an open shower and toilet just off of that room. What else could you want?

They were driven around Mo'orea in an open 4x4, and the interior of the island was lush, with waterfalls and grottos. It was there that the young island natives swam and hung out with their friends, just playing their music. Some probably thought that Pete was a gigolo accompanying a rich, older American woman, but the two of them didn't care about that. It was the most time they had gotten to spend together in years, and they were going to make the most of it.

Of course, the Tahitian islands belonged to France, so Eliza practiced her French every day. They went to a Polynesian buffet dinner cooked in an underground pit, followed by a dance show featuring the famous Tahitian fire dance. An Australian couple sitting across from them at the long outdoor table asked if they were traveling companions. Very diplomatic…. Eliza responded that they were mother and son, and everyone at the table visibly relaxed.

The announcer told the large group how they cultivated their well-known black pearls, and Eliza ended up buying a pair of black-pearl earrings as her souvenir of Tahiti. They let her pick out two black pearls from a tray, and then they mounted them later in the setting she chose. The next day they rented snorkeling equipment. Having never done that before, although Pete gave her basic instructions, Eliza gulped some seawater in the process. She was so nauseous for twenty-four hours that all she wanted to do was lie on her bed and rest.

Pete told her he would go into town that afternoon, while she napped. He came back five hours later with a tattoo on his left forearm. He didn't speak French and the tattoo artist didn't speak English, so they both had had a few beers and Pete picked a pattern from his book of tattoo pictures. It depicted birds and fish in a two-inch band of traditional Polynesian motifs that circled his arm.

He had it done in the age-old manner, with two bones – one to pierce the skin with ink, and the other to use as a mallet. Tahiti is supposedly the birthplace of the tattoo, which got its name from the *tat, tat, tat* sound that the mallet makes during the process. It was Pete's first tattoo, and as soon as Eliza was feeling better she had to admit that it looked pretty cool. On him, though – not on her.

Too soon it was time to fly back to the States, and resume their separate lives.

Eliza had her black-pearl earrings and Pete his tattoo, to remind them of the unexpected trip they had shared. *Maybe that's the best kind, despite the snorkeling mishap,* Angela decided.

Twelve

On Eliza and Pete's way home from Tahiti, when faced with an eight-hour layover in Los Angeles, they hopped on a city bus and rode to Santa Monica. They walked down the boardwalk at dusk to the famous pier, staring at the endless expanse of the Pacific Ocean. People were swimming, even in March, riding the solar-powered Ferris wheel – the first one of its kind in the world – and the roller coaster. They had dinner in a Mexican restaurant overlooking the ocean, and then raced back to the airport. They felt like a couple of kids playing hooky….

That same summer of 2004, Pete made Eliza very proud indeed when he passed his doctoral comps in Environmental Science. She decided to get busy herself, and began writing the children's book she had been thinking about for some thirty years. Soon she had finished the rough draft for an "easy reader," named *Right on Time*.

It told the story of what happens between 11 AM and 12 noon on a not-so-ordinary grandfather clock, when the minute hand visits with each number on his way around the clock to 12:00 – lunchtime!

Eliza thought she'd better elaborate a bit more in her book description: "The numbers he meets along the way all have different personalities, and stories to tell. Even the hour hand and the second hand must play their parts. This journey in time reveals unexpected relationships, rivalries, and cooperation among the numbers – and the ultimate challenge faced by the minute hand: to arrive right on time together with the hour hand at 12:00 noon. All this unfolds in the context of giving young readers fun-filled practice with the concept of telling time."

After trying in vain for many months to find a children's-book publisher for *Right on Time*, Eliza decided to self-publish it with an online publisher. That had already worked well for her family history, *The Carpe Diem Kid*, since it meant that as the author she had the final say about content and format. Her collaboration with an illustrator for *Right on Time* was also on *her* terms, and she liked it that way.

—

Summer writing always morphed into fall teaching for Eliza, however, and some forms of slave labor were still alive and well in U.S. university systems, even in the new millennium.

University slaves, also known as adjunct faculty, actually agreed to be taken advantage of by university officials in the name of education. Eliza's mentor during her first year was a fellow French prof, who was already on phased retirement from his full-time teaching job there.

He gave her a piece of good advice, knowing that she was part-time and being paid a mere pittance per course that she taught. "Don't let them give you any extra duties, outside of your classes," he said. "You're only being paid to teach, but they'll try to add things on, here and there. Don't let them get away with it." She took his words to heart, but they soon went out the window once he was gone, and she was on her own.

His words came back to haunt her, however, when she was asked to organize the French portion of the yearly foreign language competition for area high school students, that was held at the university. Of course, she would not be compensated for the extra responsibility, but who else *was* there to do it? All their other French profs had retired, and she was the only one left in the foreign language department who even *spoke* French. She caved, and didn't say no. Even Angela whispered to her that it was a big mistake.

Eliza was faced with the daunting task of finding seven to ten judges for the various events every year, all of whom had to be competent in French.

She dredged up retired French profs, French exchange students on campus, teachers from other departments who just happened to know French, and even some of her best students. She made up hundreds of quiz-bowl questions in French, and hoped that it would be enough. She worried whether everyone would show up on time, especially her student helpers. Her blood pressure went through the roof, but there was no extra compensation.

There *were* some fun times, though, like meeting a group of her students at the French bistro, *Bouchon*, in downtown Asheville for dinner, once every semester. It was on her own time, however, and Eliza even ordered some *escargots* and a bottle of wine to share with those who were interested – and were at least twenty-one! It got expensive, but she did it anyway. Maybe she could write it off her taxes, as a professional expense. It could be a hassle, though, when students changed their minds at the last minute, or left her waiting at the restaurant and then didn't show up.

All the foreign language teachers at the university offered conversation tables to their students, too, outside of class. The inequality lay in the fact that there were five Spanish professors to share the task of facilitating all their conversation tables, but only one French prof to organize the whole thing! And, of course, those five Spanish profs were all on full-time salaries, so they were getting paid for the occasional "duties as assigned."

—

What made teaching so worth the time and effort were the few-and-far-between students who were actually interested in the subject matter and who, therefore, stood out above the rest. Some students only took a foreign language because it was a requirement for their major field. Others were there because they wanted to be, and they made each class a joy for Eliza.

First came Mike, a student in his thirties, who had already served his country in the military. His goal was to take every French course she offered, in preparation for a year of study abroad in France. He was only a "C" student, but he made up for that in effort and dedication. After four semesters of French at WCU, he went to school in Angers, France, for a year and transferred enough French credits back home to graduate with a minor in French. Where there's a will….

David was a horse of a different color. He was an immature student, and a struggling musician. He challenged everything she said in class, but was one of the few students who consistently made the effort to speak French during class. It was impossible not to like David. He ended up in Nice, in the south of France, studying music and writing original songs in French. He would email Eliza his newest song lyrics, and she would make suggestions and corrections.

When David got home, he formed a group and they sang and played his music in clubs, in his home town of Charlotte, North Carolina.

Her *student* Charlotte was a fashionista, who always wore Uggs boots to class. She too aspired to study in France, and she took all four French courses offered. She was a perennial student who really didn't want to graduate, so she hooked up with the study-abroad program – and also with practically every male student she encountered on campus. She told Eliza that she had been accepted by the University of Paris and also by the Sorbonne University in Paris.

"Which one should I choose?" she asked Eliza.

"Are you crazy?" Eliza shouted, as she began pulling out what little hair she had left, after ten years of university slave labor. "You go to the Sorbonne, of course! Being able to include that on your résumé is certainly worth the extra effort you might have to put in, just to survive in class there."

Charlotte went to the Sorbonne, survived, made more than a few conquests in her short shorts – among students and profs alike – and sadly, returned to the mountains of North Carolina after her year in Paris. Eliza lost contact with her, so maybe she went back to Paris on her own after her graduation.

Other stand-out students have faded a bit in her memory now, like the girl who went to Lille in northern France to study, and posted a blog of her daily experiences. Or the boy who liked to write short stories, with whom she traded her own creative writing samples for comments and encouragement. He almost failed French, but would probably go far as a writer.

—

Eliza had various scares over the years, including being told one time by the department that they couldn't renew her teaching contract because of "budgetary constraints." This was after the new university chancellor threw away a whopping two million dollars to hire a better football coach and assistant coach. They still didn't win many games! I guess you *don't* always get what you pay for…. They paid Eliza less than anyone in the foreign language department, including the secretary, and she gave them twelve years of dedicated service, almost never missing a day of classes.

But then the tide began to turn. Eliza asked for a substantial raise at the end of the fall semester. If it were denied, she might fold her tent and quietly slip into retirement. There was more to life than lesson plans and correcting tests. She'd find something better to do at 7 AM than take her life in her hands on dark and icy winter highways. This slave laborer would write her own emancipation proclamation.

"What do you think I should do, Jon? The head of the department doesn't think that my request for a raise will be granted…."

"That's totally up to you, Eliza. I would support you either way, but you have to be able to live with the consequences of your decision." Her downhearted expression touched his heart. "Maybe it would be a sign that we should pull up stakes here, and move back north – closer to our other kids and grandkids."

"But you love it here in Asheville, and so do I!"

"I know, but our family is more important than a place. Your older granddaughters are teens already, and their parents' next baby is due in April. You're missing all the fun!"

"You mean move to Pennsylvania?"

"It would be hard to leave all the friends we've made here, but thirteen hours of travel time back and forth each way is hard on us – and hard on them, too, if they want to visit us here."

"Well, let's wait and see what the university bigwigs decide. It'll be interesting to find out how important I really am to my department…."

Thirteen

As it turned out, Eliza was denied a pay raise, but she still had to teach the spring semester in fulfillment of her contract. She told the department head that it would be her last semester, and began preparing for her classes to commence after the Christmas holidays. She was starting to feel old, or maybe it was just that her students seemed like they were getting younger and more immature. She dreamed about a few exchanges she had had with students during the first week of the spring semester:

Several students ran into her classroom as she was gathering her things to leave, at the end of her second-year French class.

"We just left Dr. Couture's beginning Spanish class, and we think we need a higher-level course. Can we register for *your* class?"

"But I teach French…."

"No, you don't!"

"Yes, actually I do!"

"Oh...."

—

When she invited the class to ask her anything they wanted to know about her, in French of course, one male student whom she had taught the previous semester asked:

"When are you going to retire?"

"Never! When are *you* going to graduate?"

He dropped her class the next day. Maybe she shouldn't have told them all that she had two granddaughters....

—

When she handed back their first French compositions, she pointed out to one boy that he had only written nine sentences.

"You were supposed to write at least ten sentences."

"You mean ten different ones?"

—

At the end of a class that was spent taking a test, a boy approached her with his paper, quite bewildered.

"I didn't finish the test. I didn't have enough time. What should I do?"

"Hand in your paper...."

—

Now that Eliza and Jon had decided to move up to Pennsylvania, she started to dream about some of the happy times they had experienced in North Carolina. Angela tried to edit out any bad memories, but she wasn't entirely successful. Into every life some rain must fall, they say, and Eliza's life was no exception.

It was 2004, and Eliza and her husband of ten years, Jon, had found their seats in the Thomas Wolfe Auditorium, and were waiting for the concert to begin. They had bought tickets for only half of the Asheville Symphony concerts this season, in an attempt to save money. They liked being able to pick their favorite music out of the line-up, too, and they were looking forward to Beethoven's Ninth Symphony this evening. Eliza particularly wanted to hear the Symphony Chorus sing the *Ode to Joy*.

They had been in Asheville, North Carolina, for several years, and had also purchased a half-season of tickets for plays at the Flat Rock Playhouse.

It was the State Theater of North Carolina. Eliza remembered how they had attended Center Stage and the Baltimore Symphony, when they lived in Maryland. Music and live theater were two of the arts that she wouldn't want to live without. Jon was happy to accompany her, although an action movie was more up his alley.

Before the concert started in Asheville, Jon leaned over to Eliza and whispered, "I think the couple sitting to me is speaking German to each other." He was right. Eliza could make out the general topic of their conversation, but she couldn't hear every word. Besides, her German was a bit rusty, to say the least. She hadn't used it on a regular basis since they had lived in Germany, four years ago. Even then, she had worked with Americans and spoken English every day.

Jon had no problem initiating a conversation with them, in English, and soon the four of them were chatting away. The concert intervened, but they continued to get to know each other at intermission. They told Jon and Eliza about the German Heritage Circle they belonged to, and how they had been offered the tickets for tonight's concert by the President of the club and his wife, who were unable to attend. They encouraged Jon and Eliza to come to one of their meetings, but that's as far as it went.

Life went on, Eliza teaching French at Western Carolina University and Jon working at the Biltmore Estate.

The next time they went to a concert, there was a different couple sitting next to them – but they were *also* speaking German! This must be the club's President and his wife, they thought, and sure enough they introduced themselves as such. Their German friends had told them to expect meeting an American couple that was interested in German. That was the beginning of a friendship that would last for ten years.

———

The President of the club wouldn't take no for an answer! They were invited to the next regular dinner meeting, as his guests. That Friday evening, Jon and Eliza approached the old stone Episcopal Church in North Asheville with some apprehension. What if everyone were speaking German? Jon only spoke restaurant German, from his travels while they lived in Wiesbaden. But you couldn't talk about *Schnitzel* and *Wasser* indefinitely!

Eliza had studied German, but that was fifteen years ago!   Besides, German literature would probably *not* be the topic of conversation tonight. The President greeted them, as he did everyone who came in, and soon they felt at ease. He introduced them all around, in English, and Jon found out that he wasn't the only spouse who didn't speak German.

Many of the men had been in the U.S. military during WWII, and had brought home German brides afterwards. Some of these same brides were now widows, but they continued to come to the meetings.

Loving to cook for more than just themselves, these women regularly prepared the main courses of each month's German dinner, and everyone else brought side dishes or desserts. The aromas emanating from the kitchen, as they walked into the church hall, were filled with the promise of a traditional German meal.

First, they all ate dinner, the eldest members being encouraged to go to the head of the buffet line. Some used canes or walkers, but their enthusiasm was undeniable. Others were younger than Eliza and Jon, though the median age was probably sixty. The menu that night included sliced pork in gravy, home fries with bacon and onions, red cabbage, and imported German pumpernickel bread with real butter. Sides included pickled herring and deviled eggs – two of Jon's favorites – tossed salads, and various cheeses with crackers. German beer and wine were plentiful.

The dessert table was filled with homemade cakes, fruit tarts, imported chocolates, cream puffs, and cookies. Jon was in his glory. No one cared if he was Irish, and couldn't speak German! He was married to a woman of German heritage, and that was enough to put him in good standing with the group. His gregarious nature endeared him to everyone, and they turned a blind eye when he began sampling the cookies before dinner was even served. In fact, some of the others followed suit!

After dinner, the business meeting ensued. The President began by introducing Eliza and Jon as his guests. This was done in English, as a courtesy to the fair number of non-German speakers present. A smattering of German and English was spoken at each table, depending on who happened to be sitting there. Eliza tried to practice her German whenever she could, and they were patient with her hesitations and mistakes.

—

Each meeting, they found out after they joined the club, centered on a different theme or activity. Everyone dressed as Bavarians for Oktoberfest, and CDs of drinking songs accompanied dinner. Sometimes a member played familiar German folksongs on the piano, and everyone sang. Other times a travel DVD took them all on a cruise down the Rhine River, and the tears flowed. For many, that was the setting of their childhood memories.

The Christmas concert of the German Heritage Circle was the most anticipated event of the year. It was held in the church proper, and soloists played the violin, flute, and organ, and some sang classical and traditional German Christmas carols. Some years school groups sang in German, and the President of the club introduced each performer from the pulpit, giving a brief background of the piece. It was like a history lesson in German music through the centuries. Sing-alongs were always the highlight of the afternoon.

Eliza was asked to read a German poem one year, and she all but memorized it as she anxiously rehearsed. Then came the *Weihnachtsmann* (Santa Claus) with his goofy elfin assistant, who distributed gifts to the children. Their names were called out, known as if by magic, and their parents and grandparents were reminded of their own childhoods in Germany. But the afternoon wasn't over yet. Everyone walked back to the hall, where the smell of hot coffee and *Glühwein* (hot mulled wine) acted like a Pied Piper or Svengali, drawing the audience in for homemade Christmas cookies and *Stollen* (German fruit loaf).

Eliza's colleague, the German prof at WCU, came one year and brought a handful of his students to experience an authentic German Christmas celebration. Unfortunately, the university was too far away for them to become regular members of the club, but they enjoyed the afternoon – especially the *Glühwein*! They heard German being spoken, outside the classroom, and attempted to join in. What more could you ask?

Fourteen

Summer was picnic-time for the German Heritage Circle. The couple that Eliza and Jon had first met at the concert hall usually hosted the annual event, since their house and front porch held the most people. They could accommodate everyone – rain or shine. They lived on the bank of a small stream, and had acres of land for walking off the picnic lunch. There were no neighbors near enough to object to the German music emanating from the house, either.

Bratwurst sizzling on the grill comprised the main course, along with German potato salad and rye bread sharing the plate with brown mustard and butter. Any vegetarians would have to content themselves with salads and desserts, but those who didn't eat meat were in the minority. The beer and wine flowed freely, and tables set up on the wraparound, covered porch accommodated everyone.

—

Eliza was anxious to practice her German, and decided to join the group of German ladies who met for lunch once a month – to eat, drink, and speak German. When she asked the organizer, a rather snobby German member of the club, about where they were meeting next, the response was unexpected.

"I don't think your German is good enough to join us, dear."

But that's precisely why I want to come, she thought. *If I were a native-German speaker, I wouldn't <u>have</u> to practice!* That stopped Eliza in her tracks, and she never joined them. But the more she thought about it, the angrier she got! She mentioned it to the President of the club, without naming the woman who had dismissed her so rudely. She didn't have to – he knew who it must have been, and he spoke harshly to her. It didn't matter, though, since Eliza wouldn't ever go where she wasn't wanted.

—

The German Heritage Circle organized a bus trip one year to an Oktoberfest celebration south of Charlotte, North Carolina. Jon wasn't interested, since he didn't drink, and that was pretty much all you did at Oktoberfest! So Eliza went with the group, and roomed with one of the other women who was also going solo. It wasn't as much fun as she had hoped, though, partly because no one had asked her to dance to the German band. She guessed that the men were afraid it would get back to Jon – but he wouldn't have cared.

The club's hard-working president finally stepped down, after more than ten years of service. He was just worn out. Unfortunately, no one wanted to take his place, and the club eventually disbanded. The Treasurer disbursed the money in the club's bank account to the members, according to how many years they had each been paying dues. Everyone would rather have kept the club going, than to receive the refund. But they didn't want to keep the club badly enough to volunteer to be president.

His shoes would have been almost impossible to fill, anyway. He had worked tirelessly to promote the German language and culture, without any pay and very little thanks. No one could have duplicated the German concert that he had orchestrated every Christmas. It was the end of an era. When Eliza got the news that Walter had died, she wasn't surprised. He had given his life's blood to the German Heritage Circle, and it was a unique moment in time.

—

About a third of the way through Eliza's years of teaching French at Western Carolina University, she had done a two-week French immersion session in Montpelier, France. Her memories of this interlude had been mostly favorable, aside from the head trauma of a fall in her dorm room a few hours after her arrival there. Whenever she dreamed about those two weeks in France, however, the dizziness she experienced as a result sometimes outweighed the language benefits.

One day, she had opened one eye, then the other – *nope, the alarm's not set – it must not be a teaching day. Halleluia!* she thought. *I can snuggle down into the covers once more.* But maybe I should get up anyway, and go to exercise class. Lots of *shoulds*, left over from my childhood, still creep into my thoughts even before I'm fully awake.

I push off the warm blankets with my feet and spring up to a sitting position, as is my habit. No crawling out of bed or snooze alarms for us morning people. On that particular Tuesday morning, however, springing was not the best idea I'd ever had. The room begins to spin wildly, as though I'm on one of those whirling cup-&-saucer rides I hate, or as if I've just awakened after a drunken orgy. I think I would at least remember participating in a drunken orgy, so that can't be it! As I grab the bedpost for dear life, I also scream for my husband to help me. I'm not sure what I think *he* can do about it, but isn't that one of the things husbands are for?

I stagger through the day, canceling plans right and left, and being obsessively careful not to look downward or lie down flat again. Each transgression thrusts me back into the twilight zone of cup-&-saucer hell, and I soon learn my lesson. My doctor agrees to see me that afternoon, and my husband and I – you don't think I'm stupid enough to drive *myself*, do you – proceed to waste away in the waiting room and the examining room respectively, for what seems like years, but is actually only a matter of hours.

"Another patient needed admitting to the hospital," a nurse explains, "and the paperwork's a pain. You understand, I'm sure." *Nothing urgent about the room spinning, of course!* After all, even "the world keeps spinning round and round," as they sing in *Hairspray*! Maybe it was participating in that dance routine with the Asheville Choral Society last month that brought on this condition! The music is certainly still going round and round in my head.

"But no," reassures the doctor, just when I'd given up hope of ever seeing him, and had read every magazine and poster in the examining room, "it's probably just a case of an inner-ear infection, and these various prescriptions will fix you right up." That's when I decided I should mention the blow to my forehead last summer, on the first day of my two-week immersion course for teachers, in southern France. I had been dizzy every morning of the two weeks after that, when I rose from bed in my hot and humid dorm room. My French doctor had blamed it on the heat – 38 Celsius.

———

"Maybe an MRI *would* be in order now," my U.S. doctor admitted, stroking his beard. "Too late today, though. Be there bright and early tomorrow."

Easy for *him* to say! Rising Wednesday morning was a replay of Tuesday, in the cup-&-saucer-hell department.

I must say, however, that the local hospital has my doctor's office beat in the area of *round 'em up and move 'em out.* Before I knew it, I was lying flat on the MRI table, dizzy as a drunken-orgy hangover victim, and sliding through the white tunnel with earplugs jammed in my ears. The noise was deafening, but I could still hear my heart pounding like a courtroom gavel. I was scared. They told me to close my eyes and not move a muscle. After fifteen minutes it was over, but then the wait began.

Sitting in the radiology waiting room, I still felt dizzy and frightened about what the results might show. Had my fall last summer addled my brains even more than they were already? Had it caused a tumor to form? The French doctor had told me that I probably didn't have a concussion, since I was speaking to him in a language that was not my native tongue. We had both laughed, but should I have trusted his conclusion?

I know I'm having more and more trouble remembering my students' names this year, but I usually chalk it up to "senior moments." Could my dizziness mean that it's more than that? After an hour of waiting for the radiologist to read my MRI, I wandered out to the reception-area hallway. The receptionist said that she was on the phone with the radiologist, so I stood there not-very-patiently waiting.

Along came a hospital bed, being pushed down the hall by an orderly. I had to jump out of the way of the speeding bed!

The female patient was sitting up in the bed, and as they passed by me she said, "Eliza?" I had no idea who she was, and the bed kept moving down the hall. The orderly looked back at me with a question mark in her eyes, and I just shrugged. It was another one of those twilight-zone moments, when people you don't recognize pop up in strange places and insist that they belong in your life. I guess I'll never know, unless she suddenly appears again sometime and asks me what I was doing in the hospital that day.

Then the receptionist called me over, and whispered the words I had been longing to hear, "Your MRI was normal." When my husband Jon picked me up minutes later, I could see the worry on his face until I told him the news. My dizziness was still unexplained, although it is fading day by day with medication. I guess my time for catastrophic illness is yet to come. We all have to die of something, but I probably won't be able to blame the French when my time comes. I just wished I knew who was in that hospital bed!

Of course, Angela knew just who it was – a German woman from the German Heritage Circle! The mystery would be solved at the next meeting, when the two members would run into each other again. Luckily, neither one of them had serious health conditions – yet. Eliza's would come fifteen years later, in Pennsylvania, just as the COVID-19 virus infection rate seemed to be slowing down at last – until the BA.5 Omicron sub-variant became the most transmissible one yet! Very few would escape its reach….

Angela also knew what was causing Eliza's dizziness. It was finally diagnosed as benign positional vertigo, although every specialist Eliza saw categorically denied that it had anything to do with hitting her head when she fell in her dorm room in France. But Eliza and Angela knew differently. Those crystals in her inner ear got knocked for a loop when her head hit the linoleum floor that late-afternoon, and they have refused to stay where they belong ever since!

Fifteen

Eliza had fond memories, and sometimes dreams, of going back to the Spangenberg Reunion in 2007, seven years after their tour in Germany ended. She and Jon took her brother's widow Mira this time, to toast his memory with good German beer and sing the songs their great-grandfather sang before he set sail for the promise of America. Their German friends, Volkmar and Liselotte Weber welcomed them into their home in Bavaria again, and first encouraged them to take an afternoon *Schläfchen* (nap). After a few days of sightseeing, they celebrated *Mutterstag* (Mothers' Day) with the Webers and then drove north from Schweinfurt to Nienhagen, to visit their other German friends, cousin Gudrun and her husband Tom Witte.

At the beginning of their second week in Germany, a joint visit to the city closest to Nienhagen – Göttingen – was in order.

There, they went to see *die Gänseliesel* (the goose-girl) statue in Göttingen's square. Two years before that, when Pete had come to the Reunion with Eliza, he had promised to return to Göttingen when he finished his doctorate and place a bouquet of flowers at her feet, next to the geese she is tending. The custom was for all local graduates to bring her flowers, and also to climb up beside her and give her a kiss. So Eliza told the goose-girl that Pete was almost finished with his degree, and then he would come and visit her, for good luck.

Mira also wanted to see the pub, once a boarding house in Nienhagen, that had belonged to their ancestors who left Spangenberg. So that evening they all went down to the bottom of the Wittes' hill for a beer.

There is no longer any evidence of Spangenberg ownership, but it's a nice local meeting place for the neighborhood. The customers, mostly men of course, filter in as the evening progresses. Whenever someone arrives, he raps his knuckles once on each occupied table, as a kind of greeting. Then he sits down with his cronies. Some people rap-around-the-room when they leave as well, but this didn't seem to be obligatory.

Gudrun and Tom had medical appointments the next morning in Northeim, so they dropped Mira and Eliza off at a local indoor shopping mall on their way. No too long ago, there *was* no such thing in Germany, but now the U.S. influence had struck again.

The big difference was that German malls had quite a few bakery/cafés nestled among the shops, for tired shoppers to stop and relax with a cup of coffee and a slice of cake. Very civilized….

Jon had already left for Frankfurt on an early-morning train, to pick up his Kawasaki motorcycle rental. His plans for the weekend did *not* include the Spangenberg Reunion, since he had already attended it three times with Eliza and he still didn't speak German. The shoppers and patients all arrived back home in the early afternoon and Julia, the Wittes' married daughter who lived in the upstairs apartment with her family, had dinner ready for them – fettucine pasta with bacon and cream sauce, topped with fresh arugula from her garden, and vanilla-crunch ice cream for dessert.

As the weekend of their last week in Germany approached, Eliza and Mira drove their rental car – a brand new, six-speed, silver, Opel Vectra – to Spangenberg for the Reunion. In a little over an hour of no-speed-limit autobahn driving, they rolled across the drawbridge of Schloß Spangenberg, in the heart of the state of Hessen. It was so fabulous that they could actually stay in *their* castle, along with all the other travel-weary Spangenbergs.

Our Tree

A long-lost cousin, newly found.
A German town
Waits patiently
With its story.

She welcomes us with happy smiles,
No thought to miles.
Three centuries
Have formed our tree.

Our castle stands upon the hill.
A grand ball still,
The spirits of
The knights do love.

Schloß Spangenberg, and the surrounding town of the same name, was founded by knights in 1214. Both were bought by Hessian Count Otto in 1350. By 1631, the Schloß had become one of the strongest Hessian fortresses, but in 1758 it was captured by the French. In the 1800s, it reverted back to the Hessian Government, and in turn it imprisoned Frenchmen captured during the Franco-Prussian War of 1870-71. This was when Eliza's great-grandfather, August Spangenberg, made his way to America. Smart young man! In the early 1900s, the Schloß was a Prussian school of forestry, and in 1945 it came under heavy shellfire at the end of WWII. It was rebuilt in 1951, and in 1985 was converted into a hotel/restaurant by the state of Hessen.

The reunion weekend's only full day of activities began with a morning bus tour to nearby Melsungen. Mira and Eliza chose the *Stadtführung* (walking tour) once they got there, rather than a boring tour of the Braun factory that makes medical equipment.

The German tour guide made a half-hearted attempt to translate some of his comments into English, but Eliza ended up interpreting his narrative for Mira and the other English speakers. She should have gotten a portion of what he was paid!

The bishop who had required the whole town of Melsungen to convert to Lutheranism, because of his close friendship with Martin Luther, would never have succeeded today given the increased emphasis on religious tolerance and diversity, according to the tour guide. They passed a mother swan sitting on her nest at a bend in the river-bank, while daddy swan stationed himself just offshore, to watch for predators. The oddest thing of all, in view of Germany's sense of order, was an old wooden door on a house. Eliza and Mira weren't sure if the door was crooked, or if it was the foundation of the house. But it certainly made them feel dizzy to look at it.

The highlight of the weekend was always the *Bal im Rittersaal* (the dance in the knights' ballroom of the castle). Everyone dressed up, and the band started out with German polka favorites. By the end of the evening, however, the lead singer was belting out old American top-40 hits, to cater to the younger generation still on the dance floor. Mira and Eliza had finished off a bottle of *Sekt* (sparkling wine) between them, not to mention the wine they already had at dinner.

Then the reunion organizers broke out the house "champagne," to celebrate the 16th Spangenberg Reunion.

That meant that these gatherings have been going on for 32 years, every 2 years since 1975. This was Eliza's sixth reunion, since she first came in 1993 with a colleague of hers. Every time, she wondered if it would be her last, but it was still six more times than her brother Laurie was able to come.

After the business meeting the next morning, Mira and Eliza hit the autobahn again in their rented Opel, this time headed for Wiesbaden to meet Jon after his motorcycle trip. They entered the address of the Hotel Oranien into the car's built-in GPS, confident that it would get the job done. When they specified their language as English, the result was a testy woman's voice with a British accent. Whenever they didn't turn the way she told them to, she obnoxiously commanded, "Make a U-turn, NOW!"

Once they were in the Wiesbaden suburbs, her directions landed them in the middle of a field, with no buildings in sight! She pompously announced, "You have arrived!" Only if they wanted to pitch a tent, and sleep on the ground! Luckily Mira had a good sense of direction, and noticed that when they had been told to turn *left,* the signs had pointed *right* toward Wiesbaden! So, off they went, back down the same road, and soon found the hotel about five miles in the opposite direction. So much for GPS accuracy!

Jon was waiting for them at the hotel, having completed his motorcycle trip to the Harz Mountains of northeastern Germany.

Eliza and Jon had stayed at the Oranien seven years ago, after packing up their household goods at the end of their PCS. Now they were getting ready to leave Germany again, maybe for good this time. The three of them wandered through the *Fussgängerzone* (pedestrian zone) after dinner, and it felt like old times for Eliza and Jon.

Then came their last full day there – Sunday, May 20, 2007, Fathers' Day in Germany. Strangely enough, fathers in Germany celebrate their day by doing exactly as they please – riding with their motorcycle buddies, or maybe meeting their friends at the local pub for the afternoon. It wasn't a family day, for the most part. So they fit right in by driving out along the Rhine River, minus their kids and grandkids and grand-dogs. Such a familiar route, past Rüdesheim with its tourist alley, past endless castles perched on the hillsides, and stopping to see the Loreley statue at the end of its peninsula in the river.

Back in Wiesbaden, while deciding on their last dinner before leaving Germany, they ended up at *Die Hütte* near the American Arms Hotel, where they had stayed when they first arrived in Wiesbaden in 1997, ten years ago. It was a fitting end to their visit, although Eliza was beginning to feel sad. Who knew when they might have the opportunity to return?

Their flights home the next morning were more of a hassle than an adventure. Their moods had changed. There was nothing to look forward to but an endless summer.

Then they thought of Autumn – not the season, but their five-year-old golden retriever who was patiently waiting for them to return. Unlike a cat, she would be overjoyed to see them, not pout for a week. They couldn't pick her up until the next morning, but that just heightened the anticipation. Then suddenly there she was, seventy-five pounds of fluffy, golden love and licks. Now they were really home, and their little pack was back together again….

Sixteen

Why do people hold onto some things, and let others go? Surely it's for sentimental value, not intrinsic.... Oh, how Eliza danced to "Broadway Baby" that spring of 2007, and sang her heart out with the Asheville Choral Society. Long past the proper age for such onstage shenanigans, she nonetheless donned her glittery silver overskirt, slit into numerous flowing strips, with matching neckpiece and head band. Her bright-yellow feather boa completed the costume, and they all became Broadway Babies as they shimmied across the stage. Now it all hangs in her out-of-season closet, permanently out of season. But you never know, she might be invited to a Halloween party some year!

Sitting at her desk in her study/guest room one early October morning, she pulled open a drawer to check a bank statement and was shocked to find it overflowing with yellow feathers! *Her* yellow boa feathers!

Being a city girl, transplanted into the mountains of North Carolina, she screamed for her husband who promptly diagnosed the situation as the nest-in-progress of a mommy field mouse. Eliza ran over to the closet, clear across the room and, sure enough, her boa had been stripped down to a mere skeleton of its former self!

How did the trespasser get in the house, the closet, the drawer? She'd probably never know, but one thing was certain – the field mouse had to go! The next morning, after having disposed of all the feathers the day before, Eliza gingerly opened the drawer again, and there were the beginnings of another nest – some stray feathers that must have fallen to the closet floor, and some bits of blue yarn. *What could <u>that</u> be from...? Of course...!* Their golden retriever, Autumn, had a fluff-ball of yarn with red, white, and blue bits sticking out. Eliza couldn't believe that mouse had searched through the house at night to find nesting materials! She wanted to meet this creative creature, but it only came out at night when the house was quiet and dark.

Eliza decided that she was smarter than the mouse – she ought to be, anyway – so she disposed of the second nest, and filled the drawer with boxes of blank checks to leave her no room to start again. Her husband outfitted some mousetraps with his precious cheddar cheese, and they retired upstairs. She couldn't bear to check the traps the next morning, so he performed the manly search. The mouse had succumbed to a midnight snack on the closet floor, and was caught.

131

Eliza had mixed feelings, but was ultimately relieved that her study belonged solely to herself again. Almost a month later, she had all but forgotten about the whole thing. Fall had finally arrived in the mountains, after a beautiful Indian summer, and the morning air was crisp again. Time to switch over her closet from summer to winter clothes. Upstairs went the winter sweaters and wool slacks, and down to the study came the sleeveless blouses and Capri pants.

While arranging her bedroom closet with teaching clothes for the upcoming winter, something blue caught her eye. Her beautiful periwinkle-cashmere-turtleneck sweater from their trip to Scotland hung in virtual shreds on its hanger, nibbled beyond repair. Their little mouse had found the two softest things in her closet, not Autumn's fluff-ball after all, but certainly two of Eliza's most cherished keepsakes. On the one hand, she couldn't blame her, but on the other, she didn't feel as bad anymore about her demise.

Angela had to laugh at Eliza's dream about the field mouse. Now that her guardian angel duties were invisible to her protégée again in Asheville, Angela had been wondering how long it would take Eliza to discover the boa feathers in her desk drawer! It really wasn't the kind of happy dream that would help Eliza cling to life fifteen years down the road, in her hospital room in Pennsylvania, but maybe more cheerful dreams were on the way.

—

Eliza did seem to be preoccupied with bananas lately…. *In our house, it's a banana a day,* she wrote in her journal – eaten by itself, cut up on cereal, sliced on pancakes or waffles, blended in a smoothie, etc. I cover the bunch with a special, green plastic bag, to keep them from ripening too fast. Who knows what's in that plastic – maybe a chemical that will end up killing us! Ironic that trying to stay healthy could somehow hurt you….

Sometimes a firm banana will be hard to open – too rubbery. I read somewhere that we should open bananas the way the monkeys do – from the bottom. Just squeeze the bottom between thumb and forefinger, and it pops open like magic! Of course, the insides of the bottom get kind of squashed that way, but if it's going in the blender anyway, who cares? The main thing is getting your daily dose of potassium, don't you know!

I hate it when the bunch of bananas I bought last weekend gets too ripe. I try to protect them from the sun shining through the kitchen window, but it's all in vain. They get brown, and mushy, and only fit for the blender. At least a smoothie changes their composition, and makes them into something palatable. My colleague at the university, Sister Evelyn, is really hard-headed when it comes to bananas. When she comes to stay overnight with us, she brings her own.

"I don't know how you can eat ripe bananas, Eliza!

"I just buy a few green ones every couple of days," Evelyn said, "and then they're always just the way I like them."

"That's because you don't have anything better to do, Evelyn. You don't have a whole house to take care of, or a husband, or a dog, or meals to cook, or music to learn for chorus and choir, or ESL lessons to plan, or College for Seniors to teach and two WCU classes to prepare for, or books to write!"

"Well, I do have five WCU classes to teach, and besides, everything *you* do is something that you've chosen to do. Nobody is twisting your arm!"

"I know. I guess bananas are pretty low on my priority list."

—

Bananas are rather like people. We start out firm and healthy and attractive. But all too soon we begin to get flabby, and no one gives us a second look. Everyone chooses the young, green bananas – thinking they'll last longer. But ripe bananas have a hidden attraction, that only a precious few can recognize. They can transform themselves, or be transformed, into new and even better entities – a smoothie, a cake or a cream pie, or even muffins.

Eliza wrote that her upbringing didn't allow her to throw away food that was past its prime, but still edible.

134

Neither should our society discount the elderly, since they have so much to give to the younger generations. Let them, and us, keep reinventing ourselves as long as we can. Who knows when an excellent banana cream pie might emerge!

—

Reinventing yourself is a lot easier when you're younger, however. A cowboy hat meant only one thing to Eliza – *not a country-western singer*, she said, *because I really don't listen to country music; not a Texan, since I've never even been to Texas; but memories of country-western <u>dancing</u>!*

Picture a forty-two-year-old divorcée, dragged kicking and screaming by her friends to a country-western bar and dance hall in Maryland, because one friend had her eye on a guy who danced there every night. This was like a foreign country to a girl who grew up making Pat Boone scrapbooks – couples two-stepping around the dance floor, all doing the same step and going in the same direction. Even so, some guys stood out from the crowd. Maybe it was the way they twirled their partners, or wore their Stetson hats down over one eye. She was hooked!

Line dancing seemed to come easy – maybe it was all those years of doing Jackie Sorensen aerobic dancing. The only thing missing was the instructor calling out the steps. But it's a question of fitting in with the crowd, at a country-western dance hall. You couldn't just wear your regular clothes.

You had to have cowboy boots and a jeans skirt – preferably a *short* denim skirt. Hats were optional for the women. Usually when you saw a girl with a big Stetson hat on, it was borrowed from her boyfriend. It was sort of a way to show everyone that he was *her* guy. There were lots of intrigues going on. Lots of jilted lovers and jealous girls. The lyrics of country-western songs really *do* portray the lives of pseudo-cowboys and cowgirls. But she still can't just listen to the music – she has to dance!

———

Most of Eliza's dreams these days had to do with her previous life in North Carolina, her most recent memories. She'd always had a real front door, as far back as she could remember. They sported the decorations of the season – skeletons for Halloween, and Christmas wreaths. But then in Asheville she felt deprived. The entrance to her home there was a sliding glass door, leading from the front deck into the kitchen.

This was very convenient for their dog, Autumn, who sat in front of the slider most of the day, looking out. She surveyed the neighborhood and let them know when a stranger approached, or even just paused on the road near their house. Other dogs had to be kept out of their yard, of course. Autumn let them know that it was *her* yard. So the glass door was a real advantage, as far as she was concerned.

Eliza wasn't so sure, however.

It sometimes felt like she was living in a fish bowl, especially when someone approached the door. Even if it was locked, they could still see her there. Of course, that worked both ways. But then Eliza couldn't just ignore the doorbell, if she was in the kitchen. It went against her private nature, somehow. Not to mention the fact that wreaths were a thing of the past, while they lived there. It just wouldn't have been the same to put a wreath on the back door, coming in from the garage….

Why Eliza was dreaming about glass doors while she lay unconscious in a hospital bed, Angela didn't really understand. She was standing by her bedside, as her nurse in Pennsylvania now. Maybe it was the same uncomfortable feeling for Eliza as having strange doctors congregate to stare at and minister to her, while she couldn't move a muscle to ask them to leave.

Seventeen

It was no mystery why Eliza dreamt so much about Autumn, though. Their North Carolina puppy became the light of their lives while she lived with them, and they considered her a member of their family. If Autumn could have told anyone the story of her life with Eliza and Jon, it might have gone something like this:

Hi! I'm Autumn, and I'm a six-year-old female golden retriever/cocker spaniel mix – yes, strange as it may seem, my mother was a cocker spaniel. I don't know for sure, of course, but I think my father must have been a golden because I look pretty much like a retriever, with a little bit of cocker in my muzzle and ears. The fur on my back is kind of curly, too, like my mother's. But I weigh seventy-nine pounds, so my humans have me on weight-control kibble that tastes like cardboard, with an occasional treat thrown in for good behavior.

From the way humans react when they see me, I guess I must be pretty cute – my brown eyes are lined all around with black, and that makes me look like I have on eye makeup. I'm very feminine, you see. Don't ask me where the purple on my tongue and my feathery tail come from, though. I've seen chows that have a tail like mine, that curls up toward me when I'm walking proud. Like humans, I probably have more than just my mother and father in me.

I'm really glad to be with my forever family – a semi-retired couple living near Asheville, who adopted me from the Animal Compassion Network and call me their grand-dog – even though life at their house is kind of boring. They don't play ball with me much, which might have something to do with the fact that I tend to run for the ball but never bring it back to them. My father didn't stick around long enough to teach me how to retrieve.

But sometimes in the summer they walk me to the pond across the main road, and let me swim. I can chase any geese I see, too. I have two beds at home: one in the family room, so I can be near them when they watch TV; and one in the living room, where I like to sleep at night or when they're at their computers down the hall. That way, I can see when they go out in the kitchen and start rustling up dinner. That'll be my time to eat, too.

But my favorite place to be is on the front deck, looking out over our yard and the neighborhood, and watching for anything that doesn't seem normal. I lie on my bench, and keep track of every car or truck that comes up the street. Some belong here but others could be delivery trucks, and I have to bark to let my family know that there might be trouble. It's one of my jobs. Speaking of which, my most important job is to get the newspaper for my family every morning.

I run up to the mailbox as soon as they let me out, and bring the newspaper back to them. They're so appreciative that I always get a treat, and it makes me very proud. Sometimes I see the paper delivery man's car coming up the street, and he hands it out the window to me. He's the only one I don't bark at, but when he's late or doesn't come at all, I feel as if it's somehow my fault if I come back empty-mouthed. I don't get a treat then, either.

—

One day, over Christmas vacation, my family started packing suitcases and bringing them downstairs next to the door. This is never a good sign, in fact it's usually a sign that they're getting ready to take me to doggy daycare. But wait, they took out one of my beds, too! Maybe they're taking me along this time! I did my happy dance to let them know that they wouldn't regret it, and it worked!

Soon we were driving down our road, and they let me stick my head out the back window to sniff all our neighborhood smells. Oh, joy! But it really got tiresome as we drove all day, and even after dark. When we stopped for the last time that day, the colder air told me that we were far from home. I soon began to sniff a familiar smell, though, and ran right up to the door of one of their kids! I've been here in Maryland before – he's nice, and he always plays with me! He has goldfish, too, and they're fun to look at, but you can't really play with them. Oh well, his big picture window is like watching squirrel TV from the kitchen, and maybe later I can chase some of them on my walk.

I was too upset to eat my food that night – weren't we ever going home again? But the next morning we piled into the car once more. Maybe we were headed home now. We only drove for a few hours this time and when we stopped, there were no familiar sniffs. My family said that we were in Baltimore, to visit another son and his family. As long as they take my bed in with the suitcases, I guess it's okay. All I really want is to be with them, wherever they are….

But when they opened the front door, all my confidence faded. They had a dog, and he looked like a pit bull/terrier to me! He barked at us but my family went in, so I had no choice. I don't think that Spanky was happy to see me, either, but I hid behind my humans and tried not to confront him. After all, it was his house, his bed, his bones, and his blanket.

Everything was cool, though, and Spanky even let me chew on one of his bones after a while. But dinnertime was a different story. I casually walked by him on the way to my bowl of food, and he whipped around and growled at me.

I'm not used to being in a house with another dog, so I really didn't know the etiquette. Spanky was quick to point it out to me, however, and after that we were fed one at a time in a gated-off area of the kitchen. I really didn't mean him any harm – I just didn't know….   We became acquaintances, probably not friends, in the next three days we spent there. He finally let me sleep in his bed while he slept in mine, and we shared his bones – some of which I heard he hadn't paid much attention to until I arrived. I can understand that…. We even played with balloons when their son celebrated his second birthday. That was fun.

—

What? We're leaving again? Just when I was starting to feel at home. This time we drove another few hours, and when we arrived just north of Philadelphia I recognized the house right away. It was another son and his wife, who had two little girls – and a white Lab named Soleil. She and I are great friends from way back in our puppy days, and we took up right where we had left off. We slept in our own beds in the kitchen together at night, and went for walks to the park together, with our humans.

We tugged on sticks together outside, and fetched balls, except Soleil brought hers right back and I just kept mine in my mouth. Why should I give it back, when I was the one who got it first? Maybe I just don't understand this game. Soleil has one blue eye and one brown eye, so maybe that gives her some special powers when it comes to playing games. Her tail goes around like a propeller when she's excited, though, just like Tuck's back in North Carolina. And that's kind of weird.

Only one night, and we're leaving again? I don't think I like this Great Polar Route. Today we drove even farther than the first day, and when we finally arrived in New Hampshire there was three feet of snow on the ground! That's what they said, anyway. I had never seen so much snow, and it was great fun romping around in it. This time when we approached the door, I was wondering who lived there and whether they had a dog, too. It was my owner's sister and her son, and – lo and behold – they, too, had a big dog.

And, horror of horrors, a fluffy cat! The only cats I had ever seen were the neighborhood variety, that I could chase whenever I saw one from my front deck. But this cat was in his own house, and *I* was the intruder. This called for a plan…. Smokey, their male German shepherd/yellow Lab mix, was bigger than me but kind of wimpy. I heard that he had been abused by his previous owner, so he was very shy. His muzzle, ears, and tail looked like a shepherd, but in between he could have been a Lab.

Very strange, but Smokey let me eat and drink out of his dishes, and play with his toys. It was great. We just hung out together, even when all the humans were gone from the house.

The cat, Oliver, was another story. He had lots of fluffy fur, the same golden color as mine, and he pretty much ruled the roost. He would jump on his master's shoulder from his perch on a kitchen stool, and liked to be carried around like a baby being burped. I was curious about him, since he seemed to be ignoring me. So I approached him and tried to sniff his butt. This works with other dogs but not with Oliver, who hissed at me and jumped up on the kitchen counter. That's when I abandoned my plan. There was a scaredy-cat under her mistress's bed, too, and two gerbils in a cage in her bedroom who didn't really interest me, so I just kept hanging out with my friend Smokey, and left the others alone.

You won't believe what my family bought me, while we were in New Hampshire! They went shopping at an L.L. Bean outlet, and came back with a new bed for me! Not that I don't appreciate it, but I can't really bunch it up to make a pillow like I can with the old one. And there's one other thing – since they found it on a pile of returned stuff, it's monogrammed with some other dog's name, *Masie*. I guess they figured that since I can't read, it didn't matter. But I heard them talking about it, so now I know. It could be worse, though. The name on the bed could have been *Buster*. As it is, I wonder if Masie is missing his or her bed….

I didn't have much time to think about it, though, because then we were off again. This time to Boston, to visit another son. *Aren't there any girls in this family?* Yet again, I was met at the door by another pooch, this one probably a distant cousin of mine. There stood Mango, an apartment-sized golden retriever. She wasn't at all golden, however, but rather a beautiful brunette. She fit perfectly in their Boston condo, and she knew it. Her fur was soft and smooth, not curling in every direction like mine. I guess that's because she's a purebred retriever. She didn't hold it against me, though, and soon we were frolicking together in the park near their house. I hadn't had this much fun since I played with my litter-mates, before we were rescued from our mean owner in Asheville.

It seems that all good things must end, however, and eventually we had to leave Mango and her family, and drive all the way back home. The Great Polar Route was quite an adventure for me, and I made lots of new friends and acquaintances. But when I got a sniff of good old North Carolina mountain air, I knew it would be great to be home again. Maybe we could make this trip an annual event, although judging from how exhausted my humans were when we finally arrived home, I'd probably better not bring up the subject for a while....

Eighteen

More and more, Angela noticed that Eliza's dreams gravitated toward memories of her past life. Was it because her body was preparing her for the next life? Angela wasn't able to predict the future. Her job was to love and protect Eliza in this life, and her happy memories were a step in that direction. They would encourage her protégée to cling to her life and her family, in the hope of being able to create even more of the experiences that happy memories are made of. Lots of Eliza's dreams had to do with singing, Angela knew….

She was singing backup before she even knew what that meant. Always in the chorus, never the soloist. To be a soloist you had to have a strong voice, and a big ego. She had neither. High school, college – always the soprano in the last row, one of the tallest girls. Eliza could "oo" and "ah" with the best of them, as the soloist belted out an aria. As long as she didn't have to sing by herself, she was fine.

There was enough pressure in the rest of her life – grades, love, graduation, her future. Chorus was where she could hide within the group, and not be personally responsible for the way the concert turned out. If she had a cold or a cough, she could just lip-sync the melody, and no one was ever the wiser. Sometimes the director seemed to be looking right at her, as though she had caught on to her ploy, but it was impossible to prove. It didn't matter much, anyway. She was only singing backup.

After college, she gave her chorus voice a rest. She was busy with other pursuits – marriage, motherhood, a teaching career. But her singing voice was always percolating just beneath the surface of her other activities. She sang to her children, sang with her French students in class, and sang with her Barry Manilow cassette as she did the evening dishes or packed lunches for the next day. She knew the day would come when she could be a backup singer again. She bided her time.

When Eliza put away her French visual aids, and stepped out of the classroom and into a government office job, she didn't think singing would be one of the perks. She was wrong. Her agency had a wonderful chorus, called The Parkway Chorale. They practiced at lunchtime, and sang at all the important agency occasions like awards ceremonies, promotions, and Christmas programs.

The choral director was a talented older gentleman, Bob Johnson, who had led the chorale for as long as anyone could remember. He was a fellow employee, with a great voice and the dedication to match. Anyone who wanted to sing was welcomed in the chorale – no audition required. She felt at home there, and became a regular member. On rehearsal days, she ate lunch at her desk and then hurried off to sing for half an hour. It energized her for the whole afternoon.

One day after rehearsal, when she had been in the chorale for a while, the director asked if she could stay for a minute. *Had she done something wrong...?* "You've been a very faithful member of the chorale," he said. "I don't know if you were aware of this, but I also direct a small chorus outside the Agency. It's called The New Century Singers. We perform in the area on a regular basis, and I'd like to ask you to join us."

"That would be quite an honor," she said, "but you know that I don't have a very strong voice."

"I know, but your light soprano voice blends very well with others. Why don't you come to one of our rehearsals, and see if you would like to be a member."

She said she would, and one evening she found herself approaching the church hall where they practiced.

It was indeed a small group that greeted her, half a dozen singers at the most for each of the four harmony parts. She was used to much larger choruses, where her voice would not stand out. There would be nowhere to hide in this group! She counted only five other sopranos – over half of them singing second soprano. She would be one of only a few first sopranos.

The director welcomed her, and she began to recognize some other Parkway Chorale members in this small group of singers. It was nice to see some familiar faces. This was like an elite group, and she felt honored and a bit scared at the prospect of singing with them. She wasn't sure she could measure up. When she found out that they were all expected to memorize their music for each concert, she was even more nervous. But everyone assured her that *she* could do it, if they could. Small comfort....

The repertoire of this group was also a little more challenging than that of the agency's chorus. Instead of well-known music, The New Century Singers would do a concert of Appalachian Christmas music, for example. The songs were still crowd-pleasers, but the director tried to broaden the audience's horizons at the same time. The other difficulties included singing with a small group of only twenty some people, and not having the comfort of being able to hold the music in your hands. If you forgot a line, you just had to try and read the director's lips as he mouthed the words.

La pièce de résistance was a concert that this chorus participated in, along with numerous other groups, at the National Cathedral in Washington, D.C. The jazz musician Dave Brubeck himself played the piano as they sang his music, all the while in awe of his very presence. If only her brother could have been there! Dave Brubeck was his idol, and her brother even played his music on the piano at home. But he lived too far away to come to the concert. All of her family was too far away to enjoy any of the group's concerts. It was a pity.

—

When Eliza and her husband went to live in Germany for three years, she had to drop out of both singing groups, but there was a new chorus waiting for her there. It was the German-American Community Choir (GACC) of Frankfurt. She and Jon went to hear their Singing Christmas Tree concert, and Eliza immediately knew that it was the right chorus for her. So she dusted off her German, and braved her first rehearsal soon after that. Lucky that she *had* some German to dust off!

What had started off as a choral collaboration between Germany and the U.S. military personnel stationed there after WWII, had begun to change in recent years as the U.S. started pulling out its troops. Now the chorus consisted mainly of Germans, with just a sprinkling of other nationalities. They were cordial to her, but not overly friendly. Fate seated her next to a German soprano named Rosemarie.

Rosemarie took Eliza under her wing, and mothered her just enough to let her know she cared. They took turns speaking German and English with each other, so that Rosemarie could practice *her* foreign language, too. Once a year the group had a choral retreat weekend. They stayed at a retreat center in the Taunus Mountains north of Frankfurt, and rehearsed their Christmas music non-stop. On their infrequent breaks, they could walk the forest trails or even take a nap. Their meals were served family style – with lots of schnitzel and potatoes….

The Singing Christmas Tree was a sight to behold! Everyone standing on a thirty-foot scaffold in the shape of a tree, dressed in tinsel-trimmed green capes, and with one brave soul at the top who was dressed as an angel. When they sang the audience's favorite, *Rudolph the Red-nosed Reindeer,* many of the singers held up stuffed reindeer that swayed with them to the music. That song was always their encore piece, by popular demand.

—

All too soon their tour in Germany was at an end, and they made their way back across the pond. After 9-11, the Washington area lost its dubious reputation as a safe place to live, however, and they retired to Asheville, North Carolina. Eliza still longed to sing, and they attended numerous choral concerts in the area. One group definitely stood in the forefront, though – The Asheville Choral Society.

Eliza had never had to audition for a group before, but she badly wanted to belong to this one. The female director sat at the piano and played, while Eliza sang a Christmas carol she had chosen. After jumping through a few more vocal hoops, she was finally dubbed a new first soprano.

In ten years, another director picked up the baton – a younger woman with lots of ideas and energy. In her first season, she took the chorus to New York City to sing at Carnegie Hall! It was a shining moment for all of them, one they had never even dreamed of experiencing. Eliza's sons and one of her granddaughters sat in the audience with some of their friends, and that meant the world to her. How could anything top that adventure?

It was magic – the lights, the house orchestra, the music, the soloists, and the combined chorus of over two hundred singers performing John Rutter's *Mass of the Children.* Eliza even bought the t-shirt that proclaimed *I performed at Carnegie Hall,* so she would never forget how far her years of singing had ultimately brought her. But maybe it wasn't over yet…. Their new choral director was making noises about taking the chorus to Italy to sing! She'd be the first one on the plane!

Angela was so proud of Eliza and her accomplishments, and she hoped that most of her singing memories had made it into her recent dreams.

She wanted Eliza to be so caught up in her new life in Pennsylvania that she wouldn't let COVID or anything else keep her from singing again. Maybe she was beyond the rigors of a high-powered chorus these days, but she could still enjoy singing with her church choir. *Use it, or lose it…!*

Nineteen

Eliza never stopped dreaming, that's for sure, but this time it had to do with wish fulfillment.... *It all began,* she dreamed, *when my husband and I were finishing up my three-year tour of duty in Wiesbaden, Germany.* I had been saving my money, which was easy to do, since our townhouse rent was being paid by the U.S. Defense Department. It certainly was burning a hole in my pocket, however, and lots of my friends were buying new cars to take home at the end of their tours. The financial attraction of shipping it across the pond as a used car, after driving it around Europe for a while, was all too tempting. We had three months to go before returning home. The time was now. *Carpe Diem.*

I had been driving a Mazda MX-6 – not a bad little sporty car, but I longed for a German sports car that would always remind me of my German adventure.

Without realizing the fatefulness of that winter's day in 2000, we blithely took a weekend drive to the German car dealership in the area that handled U.S. specifications. There it sat in the showroom, an Audi TT, looking as though it were waiting just for me. I don't remember its color, but when I sat in the driver's seat it felt welcoming – like one's own easy chair at home. The brushed-chrome dashboard made you sit up and take notice, and there was plenty of headroom, even for my 6'4" husband. The back seat was miniscule but, what the hell, there were only just the two of us, anyway.

Of course, the salesman asked if I wanted to drive it. He knew that I'd be hooked, and he was right. The 5-speed transmission shifted like a dream, and riding so low to the ground made me feel as though I should be on a racetrack. Not that racing had ever been a dream of mine…. Back in the showroom, I made one of the most impulsive decisions of my life when I said, "I'll order one," and wrote out a check for the full amount. I chose *denim-blue* for the exterior, with *dove-gray* leather seats. I couldn't wait until it came in!

That day rolled around sooner than I had anticipated, and suddenly my dream was a reality. I was driving my bright-blue TT on the German autobahn, and trying unsuccessfully to keep my speed in check. All my friends envied me, men and women alike, regardless of age. I finally had a car that embodied me – or at least who I wanted to be – sleek, sexy, and fast.

Even my license plate was sexy: ST 2000 *(read: Sexy Teacher, year 2000)*, which happened to be the plate on the top of the pile when I registered the car. Fate? I had driven my share of boring station wagons, to chauffeur my kids around. Now it was *my* turn. My grown sons couldn't believe I had paid that much for a car, but I think they were secretly proud of their Mom.

—

The adventure really began when I picked up my TT on the U.S. side of the pond. It no longer fit in as it had before – a German car in Germany. Now it had to make its way on highways filled with its American cousins: uppity Pontiacs, down-to-earth Fords, and even surly pickup trucks. It stood out like a princess among paupers. Someone asked me if a giant had sat on my VW bug, and squashed it down! It still had the rounded lines, but it was low and lean.

My TT had left the autobahns of Germany, and landed on the Washington, D.C., beltway, near our home in Laurel, Maryland. Mega culture shock! How rude these cars were – cutting in and out, honking their horns at the slightest provocation, and traveling in the passing lane for no apparent reason. This would never have happened in Germany. A slow car in the passing lane would have quickly been run over. Where were the rules of the road? It took a while for my TT to adjust, and for me to re-adjust. No sooner were we finally feeling at home, however – two years to be exact – than we decided to move south.

It may as well have been to the moon. Asheville, North Carolina, is about as different from D.C. as Germany is from the States. The D.C. beltway sported heavy traffic 24/7, while rush hour traffic in Asheville was a joke by comparison, although a welcome one. Once again, my TT was without the comfort of kindred spirits. It was pretty much in a class by itself, engulfed by pickup trucks and SUVs. Only occasionally did it spot one of its own kind: a perky red TT convertible driven by a young woman, or a silver TT Quattro with a spoiler, speeding past us on the highway.

Our German habit of signaling a turn or a lane change seemed rather quaint and out-of-place here, where most local drivers just slowed down to a crawl for no apparent reason, until they actually started to turn. When my turning signals stopped working recently, I felt naked! I couldn't let other drivers know what I was planning to do! When I informed my local Audi dealer of my plight, he asked whether I wanted them fixed. My quizzical expression made him shake his head and reply, "Most people around here wouldn't even notice if their turning signals weren't working!" I had them fixed.

After eight good years, my TT had given me 134,000 miles of very reliable driving, as I commuted fifty miles one way through the mountains of Western North Carolina.

Trucks have peppered my windshield with dings, one of them looking like a shotgun pellet had tried to penetrate it. Come to think of it, shots ring out so frequently here in the mountains, whether it's deer season or not, that it could very well have been a hunter who caused the large indentation. Now that a law has been passed here in North Carolina, granting hunting licenses to legally blind adults, anything is possible. All I know is that when shots are heard in the area of our home in the mountains, even our dog Autumn begs to come in, somehow knowing that her life is in danger. And this is a big dog, who isn't even afraid of a major thunderstorm!

—

My TT and I have been through a few harrowing experiences together, resulting in various visits to the body shop – my way of supporting the local economy. I must say that none of these incidents were strictly speaking my fault, but then again I may be prejudiced. "Riding along in my automobile…," as the song goes, my cruise control keeping me in line, speed-wise, dusk was gathering. *Wham!* A rabbit darted out in front of my TT, just inches from the wheels. No way to stop in time, but the impact messed up the lower front bumper, which had to be totally replaced, of course. How embarrassing, for me *and* my TT!

"We'll just leave the keys under the floor mat when it's done," said the body shop guy when I dropped it off. "That way you can pick it up whenever you want."

"You mean you're not going to lock it? What if you're not there for me to pay you?" These would be essential issues where we had moved from, in the D.C. area.

"No problem," he said. "You can pay me whenever you want." What a concept! It reminded me of having a house built here in the mountains, while we were still living in Maryland. When we got ready to move to North Carolina, we asked the builder where we could pick up the keys to the house. He replied that they would be on the kitchen counter when we arrived.

"You mean the house will be unlocked? With all the new appliances inside?" That's exactly what he meant. Now that we've been here a while, our D.C. habit of locking ourselves *inside* the house when we're at home has relaxed considerably. I'm even noticing a few *y'all*s and *all y'all*s creeping into my everyday vocabulary. I'm starting to loosen up – but I digress….

Now that my TT was whole again, and could hold its hood up high, life was good. I should never have let down my guard…. Arriving at the local mall to partake of some retail therapy, my TT and I proceeded to park in our usual spot, as far away from the mall as possible. But wait! A pickup with an open trailer attached was parked right next to *our* space. We were confident that we could squeeze in, however, not noticing that the sharp end of the trailer was encroaching just a tad on our territory.

As we swung in, it caught the edge of the headlight, and I heard that gut-wrenching sound of breaking glass. Over-confidence had been our undoing. I did my shopping, hoping to see the other driver on the way out. As I returned to my TT, it wasn't the pickup's owner who greeted me, but the sight of a bright orange traffic cone marking the spot where the trailer was spilling over into our space. Maybe the next car would be luckier than we were….

—

But the worst was yet to come. Driving down the main street of Candler, North Carolina one afternoon during "rush hour," I pulled up to a red light, with the afternoon sun squarely in my eyes. The pickup in front of me was already stopped for the light, so I wasn't worried that I wouldn't be able to see when the light ahead turned green. I would just follow his/her lead. As soon as I saw the pickup moving forward, I followed suit, and found my TT driving over a step ladder that had been lying lengthwise in the road – under the pickup! The driver had to have known it was there, as he/she waited for the light. But since the pickup could easily clear it, the driver obviously felt no need to come back and warn *me* about it.

By the time I heard the screech of the ladder as my TT tried to drive over it, it was too late. The ladder was stuck under my low-slung TT, and no amount of moving forward or backward could dislodge it.

Of course the flow of traffic behind me was disturbed, and so were the other drivers! A young guy standing in the bank parking lot next to the intersection came over to my car, and suggested that I slowly turn the corner into the lot, just to get out of the way. That was the longest thirty seconds of my life, as we inched forward – my TT, me, and the ladder!

Once in the parking lot, my young advisor and an older guy decided to jack my car up so they could pull out the ladder.

"Wait! Let me take a picture as you're pulling it out. My insurance company will never believe this. *I* don't even believe it!"

The next incredible thing was the sight of the two guys fighting over the ladder! One finally gave up, because he already had a ladder, and the young guy had the decency to ask me if *I* wanted it. *Are you kidding?* All I wanted was to limp home, not that there's any space in a TT to carry a ladder anyway. So it was back to the body shop again, to replace the same front bumper. This was getting expensive, given my high deductible, and my TT was getting tired of so many face-lifts.

Soon we were on the road again, however, good as new. My one-hour commute gave my TT lots of highway exercise, but it could rest for four hours or so in a quiet parking lot while I taught my classes.

One day it wasn't so quiet though, and I could hear the weed-whackers buzzing outside as I worked in my office between classes. A frantic phone call from the department secretary sent me running outside! One of the workers had reported a flying rock hitting my TT! They pointed to the previously damaged windshield, that I had never bothered to fix, since the ding wasn't in my line of sight. The campus police arrived to write up the report, and they asked me to walk around my car and point out any new damage from the weed-whacking.

That's when the wily serpent of temptation came out of nowhere and reared its ugly head. I could actually get my employer, the State of North Carolina, to replace my whole windshield! I cursed my parents under my breath, for making me such an honest person. I just couldn't do it. But I did find some minor scratches on the side panel that weren't there before. Back to the body shop, to the tune of $150. At least it wasn't *my* $150 this time.

So, my beloved TT was starting to show its age, but so was I for that matter. Occasionally the hub caps would fly off *en route*, recently three in one week! Or a tire would pop, and then pop again the same day, after it had been "fixed." My TT didn't have a built-in CD player, so I made do with a portable one, necessitating endless wires and hook-ups. The hatch didn't open all the way anymore, just as *I* couldn't touch my toes as easily as I used to. I became rather attached to the ding in the windshield, however, and would probably have missed it if it were suddenly fixed.

It was getting harder and harder to get into and out of my low TT, but what the hell. When we were on the road together we both felt young again, as though we were still zipping along on the German autobahn – just my TT and me.

Twenty

But Eliza wasn't out of the woods yet –
physically or emotionally. As her body still lay in a
hospital bed in 2022, and her brain was still in a coma
due to COVID, her dreams began to reflect her fear of
being lost forever. Angela tapped into one of these
dreams, and was worried about Eliza's state of mind
as her protégée tried to transfer her thoughts to her
guardian angel and friend.

"I never dream of being chased by a
monster, or anyone else for that matter. I
think that would be preferable, though, to
my usual dream of just being lost. I don't
have that dream every night. Sometimes
months go by, but then there it is again.
The surroundings change, but that sinking
feeling is always there – not a familiar
face in sight, no one who understands my
feeling of panic, or in whom I can confide.

"I'm on my own…. Actually, I think being chased might be a less scary dream, in the long run – no pun intended. At least when the monster catches you, it's over. Maybe forever. But being lost never reaches a conclusion. I never find my way home, or out of the situation. I just keep stumbling or driving around, feeling more and more desperate – and then I wake up.

"It's a horrible beginning to the day, and it sometimes colors my waking hours with shades of gray and black. Luckily, I hardly ever have these dreams two nights in a row. I guess my subconscious protests to the dream gods, and they in turn decide it would be more fun to let me regain a false sense of security and confidence, before they lower the boom again…."

Angela hated to watch Eliza giving in to her feelings of hopelessness and desperation. She stood by her side as Eliza's nurse, and she knew that her patient could subconsciously hear her words of comfort and encouragement. "Eliza, you're not alone. I'm right here with you, and I won't let you get lost ever again. I'm taking care of you, and I won't give up until you come back to us – to Jon and to your family.

"But it's not only me, Eliza. You've had other angels in your life, too, without even knowing it. The first one is right here with me now – her name is Rosemarie."

Eliza heard the name Rosemarie, and her mind wandered back to Frankfurt and the German-American Community Choir. "Rosemarie? I can see your face! Is it really you?" In her thoughts, she was right back there again.

"It's really me, Eliza, in my human form. We had fun singing together, didn't we?"

"Yes, we did! You befriended me when I didn't know a single person in the chorus that first night at rehearsal. I was a lost soul, and you found me. Thank you, Rosemarie...."

"You're welcome, Eliza. We angels were made to help people in their time of need, but I never expected it to be so much fun! That Singing Christmas Tree was a hoot! By rights *I* should have volunteered to be the angel on the top of the tree, but I'm afraid of heights, so...."

"You're kidding! How do you fly around, then?"

"Well, we just appear to, and disappear from, people – like Gabriel appeared to Mary the Mother of God. Not really any flying involved.... You need to get well, Eliza, so you can sing again. Your choir at church needs you."

"I know. I'm the only first soprano, if you can believe it...."

"I believe in *you*, Eliza. If you come back, maybe I can come sometime and sing soprano with you. You never know."

"I'll try, Rosemarie. I really will...."

—

"I'll go next, Angela – while Eliza is still hallucinating."

"Oh, really? And whose form are you taking *this* time?"

"You know as well as I do that I was Bashir, Eliza's friend and confidant in Tunisia. She'll recognize me right away, Angela."

"Okay, see what you can do to coax her back to her life on earth. Maybe she has a soft spot for you...."

He appeared to her as Ridha's right-hand man in Tunisia, who had taken such good care of her during one particular program review in his country. "I hear that you are a bit under the weather again, Eliza. Maybe I can help.... *Puis-je vous aider?*"

"Is that you, Bashir? You're the only one who always spoke French to me. Come closer, so I can see you...."

Her smile said a lot, without saying a word. Bashir offered her his hand, as he always had. *"À votre service, Madame."*

"It *is* you, Bashir! You look the same, but I'm quite a bit older, I'm afraid…."

"Angels can change their appearance to fit the circumstances. This is the way I knew that you'd remember me, Eliza. Time and age have no meaning for us in heaven."

"You were a life-saver for me when I arrived in Tunis with a sprained ankle, Bashir. You took care of me, and made sure that I didn't miss a thing that week. Thank you…."

"I would like to save your life again if I can, Eliza. It's time for you to rejoin your family had friends – those you love, and those who love you. You have much more of life ahead of you, if you choose to live…."

"It won't be easy, Bashir. I'm pretty far gone already."

"Since when did you ever give up on yourself, just because it was the easy way out? You could have stayed home in Wiesbaden with that sprained ankle, and nobody would have blamed you!"

"And missed seeing my favorite ETC country again? That just wasn't an option!

"Nothing could have kept me off that plane – nothing!"

"That's the spirit, Eliza! I want you to tell me that nothing's going to keep you in that hospital bed, either!"

"I don't think it's *my* decision, Bashir…. Your Big Boss might have the deciding vote." The smile was gone from her face.

"What if He left it up to *you* – sink or swim? You'll never know unless you try…. Just think about it."

———

Angela was proud of her fellow angels, for doing their best to encourage and inspire Eliza. Angela still had an ace up her sleeve, though, in the form of one last angel who just might make the difference between life and death to Eliza, but Angela wanted to let Eliza's family talk to her first.

Her husband Jon was now permitted to be a regular visitor to the ICU, since Eliza had regularly tested negative for COVID, and he began to talk to Eliza about their life together in Pennsylvania. Even though her eyes were closed and she lay motionless in her bed, Jon took the chance that some of his words might just be getting through to her.

"You know that I wasn't in favor of our move here from North Carolina almost five years ago, Eliza. I guess that's an understatement, isn't it? I told you that I'd give myself a year to settle in, before deciding if it had been a mistake for me. Now it's been five times that long, and we're still here…. I know why you wanted to come – to be closer to your kids and grandkids, and we certainly have accomplished that, but what a roller-coaster ride it's been! After just two years here, COVID shut everything down for *another* two years, and now we were just starting to get back to a normal life….

"That's when you got hit with the Omicron BA.5 sub-variant – the worst one yet, since it's the most transmissible and the most immune-evasive variant so far. You had taken every precaution, Eliza, but it just wasn't enough to keep you safe. I'm so sorry *you* have to suffer, honey – it should have been me…. I'm the one who insisted on going out every day, even during the lockdown. I'd just put on my helmet and go for a motorcycle ride. I'd still have to buy gas and make pit-stops, but I just wore a mask inside and took a chance.

"I finally got a mild case of Omicron, but nothing as serious as yours, Eliza. Please forgive me for putting both of us at risk – I just want you to come back to me, honey, and I promise to do better…." Jon wasn't supposed to kiss her, so he just squeezed her hand as he turned to leave. Eliza subconsciously recognized his touch, and was comforted. That's all she could do.

Angela smiled, and put her own hand on his shoulder. She knew that he was hurting, too. They all were….

—

Jon planned to get some coffee at the cafeteria and visit her again before going home, but her sons Pete and Chris met him in the hallway. "Can we see her, Jon?" Pete asked. "I just drove up from Maryland, and I'll stay overnight with Chris. Is she any better…?"

"Not really. She's still in a coma, but her nurse encouraged me to talk to her, anyway. Something you say might at least let her know that you're here. Angela told me that you can go in one at a time, for just a few minutes. I'll get us coffee, and meet you both back in the waiting room."

"Go ahead, Pete," Chris said. "I'll go help Jon with the coffee."

When Pete came into her room and introduced himself to Angela, she smiled at him. She had heard a lot from Eliza about her two sons. "Just sit down next to her, Pete, and speak from your heart." Angela stepped into the hall for a few minutes.

"Ma mère, it's Pete." He used his pet name for her, and she smiled inside. "I have some happy news for you. Kelly and I got married!

"We just couldn't wait for COVID to be over, so we had a very small ceremony by Greenbelt Lake. We'll have a big wedding reception when you get out of the hospital, *ma mère*, and then we'll have *two* reasons to celebrate! I love you very much…."

Angela stepped back into the room. "Chris is here to say hello, Pete, and Jon is in the waiting room." The boys hugged each other as they exchanged places by Eliza's side. Angela hoped it wouldn't be too tiring for her, but she knew how much Eliza's sons meant to her.

"Hey, Mom! It's Chris, your baby boy! I guess that's what I'll always be to you, but now you have four grandchildren as you know, so I'll have to be a good Dad, too. We all love you so much, Mom, and want you to get well as soon as you can! Wes is two years old already, and he needs to see his 'Nanny' coming to visit him and the girls very soon. I know that you can whip this new COVID into submission, as soon as you show it who's boss – and that's definitely *you*, Mom! We love you lots…."

Chris had tears in his eyes as he left his mother's side, and Angela put her arm around him. Nurses were supposed to be professional, but she was a guardian angel first and foremost and she felt almost as though they were her own sons, or at least godsons.

Angela and Eliza had been through a lot together during Eliza's entire life, even before Angela had made her presence known. This was one angel who wasn't about to give up on her protégée….

Twenty-one

Angela had saved the most influential angel for last – Eliza's good friend and former Western Carolina University teaching colleague, Sister Evelyn. Eliza had thought it was a coincidence that she and Evelyn were hired to teach in North Carolina at the same time. It wasn't…. Evelyn had known that Eliza would need a confidante and partner in crime in the Foreign Language Department, so she threw her hat in the ring as a Spanish instructor as soon as Eliza applied to teach French. They hit it off right away, and Eliza had no idea that Evelyn would be an angelic presence in her life for the next ten years or so.

Sister Evelyn in human form was a force to be reckoned with, as Eliza soon found out when they began the school year together in 2002. Far from the stereotype of a compliant member of the religious order of the School Sisters of Notre Dame, Evelyn was happy living pretty much on her own near the campus in the Blue Ridge Mountains.

Aside from deducting her meager monthly expenses from her paycheck, Evelyn was required to deposit the balance into the religious order's bank account. They were strapped for money at the Motherhouse in Minnesota, since fewer young women were entering their convent and earning money for their survival.

Evelyn and Eliza were supposedly born in the same year, and were both in their mid-fifties when they met on campus. Evelyn's whole existence as an angel was faith-based, however, while Eliza had not been a practicing Catholic since her divorce and remarriage. That was about to change when Evelyn appeared in her life. She wasn't shy about speaking her mind, that's for sure. "Have you found a church in Asheville that you like, Eliza?"

"Well, Jon isn't Catholic, so it hasn't been a priority, I guess."

"I didn't ask about Jon – I asked about you…."

"I kind of stopped going to church when my first husband left me, Evelyn. I just felt lost, I guess."

"And how long ago was that, Eliza?"

"About fifteen years or so."

"So you turned your back on God, just when you needed Him the most?

175

"Probably not the smartest thing you've ever done – not that I know you very well, Eliza."

"I just felt alienated from a God who would let that happen to me, that's all."

"God isn't responsible for what happened, Eliza. I suspect that your previous husband was, but God had a better plan for your life all along. Am I right?"

"Well, not at first, but after I got myself back together…yes, He actually did."

"You didn't do *that* alone, either. He's been there all along, just working in the background and waiting for you to turn to Him."

"Okay, you win, Evelyn. Jon and I did go to Mass recently at a church I liked – St. Eugene's in Asheville."

"Aha! I rest my case!"

—

Now that Eliza had been struck down by COVID twenty years later, Evelyn used her angelic powers to speak to Eliza in her dreams. "Do you remember me, Eliza?" Evelyn had aged her human appearance enough to look more like Eliza's contemporary.

"Evelyn, is that you? You look a lot older than you did in North Carolina."

"So do you, Eliza. Let's face it, we're both in our seventies now – except I don't usually have a human body. I'm an angel, Eliza, and I wanted to talk to you about your life now…."

"What? Is it almost over…? All I do is dream about the past, because I can't get out of my hospital bed in the present."

"I know, and that must be the pits! You're going to need a strong will to live, if that's what you want to do, Eliza."

"I do want to live, Evelyn, for Jon and for my boys! I have four grandkids now, and I want to be part of *their* lives, too. Jon shouldn't have all the fun without me!"

"You're right! You deserve equal time, and that's why you have to fight to get better!"

"Are you really an angel, Evelyn? Why didn't you tell me before this? All this time I've been thinking about you being back in Minnesota…."

"It's too cold out there! When I left North Carolina, I went back to the celestial choir for a while, until Angela told me that you needed my help."

"She's my guardian angel, and she's been very good to me."

"Then do yourself a favor, Eliza, and hang on to your life with everything you've got! Don't give up, like so many others have done. Let's say a prayer together, and ask God to spare your life this time."

"Maybe having an angel on my side will tip the scales in my favor…."

"You've got *four* angels on your side, Eliza – Angela, Rosemarie, Bashir, and me!"

———

Not everyone believes in miracles, of course, but Eliza's four angels pulled one off that night – with God's permission, and Eliza's perseverance. The night-duty nurses noticed it first – Eliza gradually began to awaken from her month-long coma by starting to mutter words that didn't make any sense to them – *not…lost* – *not…any…more*, over and over. They called Angela, as Eliza's head nurse, and of course she appeared immediately. Guardian angels are always on call. "Has she opened her eyes yet?"

Eliza heard Angela's voice, and slowly opened her eyes for the first time in over a month…. Everything was blurry at first, but then Angela came into focus – dressed in her nurse's uniform! "Angela! What…?" she rasped.

Angela smiled and took her hand. "I'm your nurse, Eliza. I've been looking after you the whole time you've been in the hospital with COVID. Just rest now, and we'll call Jon. He's been here every day, sitting with you…."

"Long…?" she managed.

"You've been in a coma for many weeks, Eliza, but now you've come back to us. Thank God!"

After Eliza's doctor examined her, the nurse's station notified Jon that she was semi-awake, and he hurried in. "Eliza, welcome back," Jon whispered in her ear as he sat beside her. "I've missed you so much!" Angela left them alone for a few minutes. Humans liked privacy on such occasions, she had noticed. There was plenty of time to talk to him about her real relationship to Eliza, but for now it was enough for him to know that God had spared her life.

—

Then the real work began for Eliza. Angela was in the forefront, encouraging her to get moving as soon as possible – out of bed and into a chair, to regain her strength. It took time to relearn other basic movements, too, like how to stand on her own, brush her teeth and hair, and feed herself while holding cutlery. Taking a shower was especially challenging.

"Just pretend you're a toddler who's learning all these things for the first time," Angela told her, when Eliza was reduced to tears of frustration one afternoon.

"Or an angel!" Eliza stuck out her tongue.

"*Or an angel* is right!" Angela laughed. "One who has a human body all of a sudden…." Angela made sure that no one else was in the room when she said that, but then Jon walked in.

"Jon…come in!" Eliza held out her arms for a hug. "Angela…tell him now?" For a linguist, it was hard to be reduced to simple questions and answers without exhausting her vocabulary, and her energy!

"Tell me what?" Jon wanted to know, and they both looked over at Angela.

Angela nodded. "Jon, it's time for you to know that I'm more than just Eliza's nurse, and friend – I'm actually her guardian angel, and I *have* been ever since she was born. I waited to reveal myself to her in human form, though, until she went to Berlin on temporary duty thirty-some years ago. My job was to protect her in her overseas travels, and now it's to help her recover from her bout with COVID."

"Wow! It's been obvious that you two had a special bond, Angela, and I'm thankful for it – especially now! I'll do everything I can to help Eliza get back to normal, too.

“We can be The Three Musketeers!” he smiled, pretending to draw his sword.

“All for one, and one for all!” Eliza was really getting into it….

Twenty-two

It wasn't long before Angela called in her back-up angels for assistance with Eliza. First up was her fellow soprano from the German American Community Choir, Rosemarie. She remained invisible, but helped Eliza with her speaking voice through breathing exercises and singing carols they both knew. "Let's sing *Silent Night*, Eliza, like we did for the Singing Christmas Tree in Frankfurt," Rosemarie whispered in her ear. Angela had to laugh when Eliza started taking deep breaths and slowly singing *Stille Nacht* in German. It did help, though.

"When you go home, will you return to singing in your church choir, Eliza?" Rosemarie asked.

"I hope so…. Will you come and sing with us, Rosemarie?"

"If I'm not needed somewhere else – maybe just as a visiting friend."

"That would be so cool! You could be my German friend…from Frankfurt – from the choir."

"I'll always be your friend, Eliza…."

—

The angel that Eliza knew as Bashir, from Tunisia, came invisibly to the hospital next. He had helped Eliza to get around Tunis twenty-some years ago, when she arrived for the yearly program review with a severely-sprained ankle. This was an entirely different mobility challenge for her now, but he would get her moving somehow.

"Can you guess who I am, Eliza?" Bashir asked, in his accented English. "You can't see me this time, but I'll help you get out of bed and we can take a walk together." Angela positioned Eliza's walker, and gave her a wink.

"You can't fool me, Bashir – I'd know your voice anywhere! I wish I could see you, though." Angela nodded, and Bashir appeared visibly by her side in the uniform of an orderly.

"À votre service, Madame," he said, staying close by. Her first steps with the walker were hesitant, but Bashir was as patient with her as ever. "Shall we take a turn around your suite, Madame?"

That was a gross exaggeration of the space in her room, but she played along. She was just so glad to get out of bed.

"I would like to peruse my villa, Bashir, if you would be so kind…."

"Your wish is my command, Madame." They made an odd couple walking slowly down the hall together, Bashir on high alert for anything Eliza might need.   The nurses wondered where this handsome new orderly had come from, but they were too busy to ask. Angela was in charge of Eliza's care, anyway, and her smile set their minds at ease. He must be a new hire.

"I'm tired of this walker, Bashir!" she told him, when they passed her room the second time. "I want to use a cane instead."

"Not my decision, Eliza.   Let's ask Angela…."

"She can graduate to a cane when she's discharged," Angela told him, "and that depends on her doctor. Just keep walking, you two…."

"Angela's a slave driver," Eliza decided. "Not nearly as accommodating as Ridha was, in Tunisia. Is he still managing the ETC project there?"

"No, he finally went back to police work, and so did I. It just wasn't the same after you left Germany, Eliza."

"How can an angel fire a gun, Bashir?"

"The same way a decent human being does – only in a threatening situation. I'm lucky to be assigned to Ridha as his guardian angel, so there are no gray areas."

"When you see him, tell him that I miss him. He's *my* definition of a decent human being...."

—

Sister Evelyn had been one of Eliza's best friends in North Carolina, and she accepted Angela's invitation to come to the hospital and give Eliza an angelic pep talk. She took the form of an invisible voice in Eliza's ear, but there was no mistaking the mid-western lilt in her voice. "So, I heard that God saw fit to spare your life this time, Eliza. Have you thanked Him for it?"

"Evelyn? Where *are* you?"

"Just because you can't see me, doesn't mean I'm not here. You believe in *God*, don't you?"

"Of course, and now I believe in angels, too."

"Good, I'm invisible because the hospital is clamping down on visits to the ICU by non-family members. But you didn't answer my question about giving thanks to God...."

"Let's do it together, Evelyn. It'll mean more if you join me."

"I'm not sure that's true – I've always been one of His think-outside-the-box angels – but this is something important. Let's bow our heads in His presence."

"Lord," Eliza began, "You have filled my life with Your blessings, even in what I thought were my darkest hours. You always had a better plan for my life than I did, and in time I came to agree with You. Now You have literally pulled me from the jaws of death, with the help of Your angels, and I thank You most humbly. Show me Your plan for the rest of my life, and I will make it my own. Amen."

"You're a natural, Eliza – you would have made a great nun!"

"I know, but my husbands kept getting in the way. I guess *they* were part of His plan for me, too. Speaking of which, here come my boys for a visit…. Thanks for praying with me, Evelyn. It's because of you that my faith was restored, too."

"I'll take my leave for now, but don't forget – firm bananas are much better than ripe ones!"

—

Eliza was finally discharged from the hospital, and eventually from a rehab facility, too.

As Angela had promised, she graduated from a walker to a cane, and then was at long last able to walk on her own. Jon pledged to take good care of her at home, and to take every precaution against either one of them being re-infected by some other form of the virus. They both knew that there were no guarantees – of anything in this life. You just played the cards you were dealt, and trusted in God to see you through the rough spots.

Angela hung up her nurse's uniform, and went back to being Eliza's invisible guardian angel. Eliza herself returned to her regular routine of reading, writing, singing, and exercising. Since the COVID onslaught had begun over two years ago, about half of the choir members in Eliza's church had dropped out for some reason or other. One Sunday morning, however, the choir director began rehearsal by introducing a woman who had just come in.

"We have a new first soprano joining us! Her name is Rosemarie Wietschorke, and she has just moved here from Frankfurt, Germany. Eliza, I know you'll be particularly happy to finally have another soprano to help you sing the descants. Maybe you can take Rosemarie under your wing…."

Angels

I sit and wait, does an angel contemplate my fate?
And do they know the places where we go
When we're grey and old?
'Cause I have been told
That salvation lets their wings unfold,
So when I'm lying in my bed,
Thoughts running through my head,
And I feel that love is dead, I'm loving angels instead.

And through it all, she offers me protection,
A lot of love and affection,
Whether I'm right or wrong
And down the waterfall, wherever it may take me
I know that life won't break me, when I come to call,
She won't forsake me, I'm loving angels instead.

When I'm feeling weak,
And my pain walks down a one-way street,
I look above and I know
I'll always be blessed with love.
And as the feeling grows,
She breathes flesh to my bones,
And when the love is dead,
 I'm loving angels instead.

-Josh Groban, 2020

Susan Larmon (susanlarmon@yahoo.com)

Published works:

Fiction

-**Time Travel 101** (a trilogy: **Swan Songs, Spy Songs,** and **War Songs**)

-*Vive Les Vacances!* (a trilogy: **Total Immersion, Russian Roulette,** and **Father to Son**)

-**Ellie's Opal** (autobiographical fiction)

-**Memorial Service** (a trilogy: **Memorial Service, Being a Friend,** and **A Friend in Need**)

-**Spy Girl** (a double trilogy: **Spy Girl, Sheer Pretense, Collision Course, The Jasmine Connection, Practice to Deceive,** and **Danaë**)

-*Ciao*, **Bella!** (a trilogy: *Ciao,* **Bella!,** **Never Did Run Smooth,** and **A Tangled Web**)

-**Fireworks in Quebec & Body and Soul**

-**Cinderella Summer** (a trilogy: **Cinderella Summer, Cinderella Rewind,** and **Cinderella Fast-Forward**)

-**Nadia's Quest & Jeremie's Dilemma**

-**Up In Smoke & Back Down To Earth**

<u>Fiction</u> continued:

-Death in Tahiti (**Never As It Seems, Root Of All Evil, Tramps Like Us,** and **Olivia Takes Wing**)

-Front Window (a trilogy: **Front Window, That's Amore,** and **Ratsstube**)

-Second Chances (a modern-day morality play) and **Love of My Life**

-Angels Instead (autobiographical fiction)

<u>Non-Fiction</u>

-The Carpe Diem Kid (a family history)

-The Wiesbaden Years: Through Rose-Colored Glasses

-Golden-Age Reflections

-Prompt Me!

-Moments in Time (short stories)

<u>For Children</u>

-Right on Time (an easy reader)

<u>*Acknowledgements*</u>

The author wishes to thank:
Carol Loughridge and **Shirley Brown**
for their invaluable editing skills.

<u>*Bibliography*</u>

-**Angels** (sung by Josh Groban)
-from his 2020 album, **Harmony**
-written by Robert Williams & Guy Chambers

-"Riding along in my automobile…" (sung by
Chuck Berry)
-the first line in his song,
No Particular Place to Go
-written by Chuck Berry, for his 1964 album,
St. Louis to Liverpool

-**The Carpe Diem Kid** (written by Susan Larmon)
-the author's family history
-published in 2009

-"All for one, and one for all;
united we stand, divided we fall."
-These famous words from the well-known
1844 novel, **The Three Musketeers**,
by French author Alexandre Dumas,
are the motto of the three heroes –
Athos, Porthos, and Aramis – in a
swashbuckling tale of chivalrous
swordsmen who fight for justice.

* 9 7 9 8 3 5 4 0 3 9 6 0 9 *